You are the Light!

Carol

Jezebel

Queen of Darkness, Queen of Light

CAROLE M. LUNDE

JEZEBEL
QUEEN OF DARKNESS, QUEEN OF LIGHT

iUniverse books may be ordered through booksellers or by contacting:

iUniverse
1663 Liberty Drive
Bloomington, IN 47403
www.iuniverse.com
844-349-9409

ISBN: 978-1-6632-1422-5 (sc)
ISBN: 978-1-6632-1423-2 (e)

Print information available on the last page.

iUniverse rev. date: 12/28/2020

INTRODUCTION

Jezebel stood in the window of her palace just before she was pushed to her death. The "woman in the window" is a motif depicting a woman of power. In the Book of Judges, Sisera's mother was said to be sitting in the window of her palace watching for her son to return from the battle with Deborah and Barak.

What was their power, their position, and how did it fall to them? We know from the Hebrew Bible Jezebel was the daughter of King Ethbaal of the city states of Sidon and Tyre. They were Phoenicians, a sea faring people, and Baal was their god. Astarte was their goddess. They represented love, prosperity, fertility, and good harvests.

It is reasonable to believe because she was a Phoenician, Princess Jezebel was educated, talented, and quick witted. It remains to be understood why she is so reviled in the Hebrew Testament. Researchers believe it is because she was a woman of royal power, having vast legal and business knowledge. It is odd they reviled her because Phoenicia was not considered foreign, but a beneficial neighbor.

The Bible authors avoid giving her the title of Queen, even though she is the queen, being married to King Ahab. Other objections are her devotion to Baal and Asherah or Astarte. All foreign wives of kings were allowed to bring their religion with them. The kings provided appropriate places of worship for them. But Elijah the prophet was determined to establish Yahweh in the land of Israel. Yahweh was strong in Judah, but not in Israel.

She is called evil and this characterization is expanded in the Book of Revelation 2:20, where her name becomes a symbol of all the vilest and most terrifying of evils men can apply to women, even insulting her with accusations of whoredom. A popular song called her a devil. There is no evidence she was ever unfaithful to King Ahab.

She was once a child, a daughter, growing up in the privileged world of royalty. She was the apple of her father's eye and the hope of the future of the royal family. She grew up in a world where women were forced into political marriages so their families or their countries could gain greater power. Is it any wonder she would feel the sting of being sent to a backward place so unlike Phoenicia, and be reviled by the xenophobic population there?

Note: Rhacotis is the city in Egypt that existed on the shore of the Great Sea before Alexander the Great absorbed it into the founding Alexandria in 324 BC.

Chapter 1

"Father, please take me on the ship with you next time you travel. I want to know how to sail a ship! I want to see where you go and learn everything you do. I want to meet kings and queens and see their lands. Please, Father, take me with you!"

"Someday, my dear. Someday when the time is right."

Jezebel tagged along, dogging her father's steps wherever he went. She wanted to hear everything he said and watch his facial expressions. She wanted to stand tall like him and feel the same power coming through her.

Her bearing was already regal and her chin haughty as she always held it high. She might be considered a young beauty except for her steely eyes and abrupt manner. She was tall for her age, towering over the kids in the palace.

Her long raven black hair swung behind her as she walked up and down the halls. She stamped her foot when someone crossed her and stared them down with her snapping dark eyes.

She ignored the moony stares from the boys and the leers from the men in the military. She was Princess Jezebel, a favorite of her father, King Ethbaal, and she knew she was destined for great things.

Her tutor, Haman, was from Sidon. He traveled to many countries, to Egypt and exotic eastern lands, and learned from the most brilliant minds. He brought thrilling lessons and stories to her and she was eager for the next one and the one after that.

He had a crooked foot from birth and walked with a crutch, but no one seemed to notice or care. His wit was razor sharp, his smile quick and warm, and he was well liked. He was Jezebel's dearest friend and she loved him. When she wasn't following her father as he attended to his duties, she could be found sitting with Haman listening to his stories and asking him volumes of questions.

"My dear little Jezebel, I taught you from the beginning to ask questions. Did I forget to tell you to then be quiet and wait for the answer?"

"I am sorry, Haman. I will try to be patient. But it seems there is so much to learn and I want to know it all before it is too late!"

"Too late? When is it too late, Jezebel?"

"It will be too late when someday I am forced to marry a foreign ruler and even be a servant to his other wives. I want to prove I am as smart as any man! I will beat them all at their political games. I am a princess and soon to be Queen Jezebel!"

She jumped up and paraded around the room in her best queenly style.

"Be at peace, Jezebel. Come and sit down. Let us be the princess before you become a queen. There is no need to rush ahead. I will be your teacher wherever you are as long as I am alive. That is your father's command to me."

She sat down beside him and picked up her tablet and stylus. Haman placed before her a tablet with Phoenician characters or letters.

"Why must I draw these funny lines? What are they for?"

"They are called hieroglyphs or pictures of the letters. When you put them together they make words. When you go to the palace stores, ask the servant to see the list of items in the store rooms. You will see them on the list and he can show you what items they represent."

"If the servants can make them, why do I have to learn them?"

"You must learn to recognize them so no one can cheat you. You will see your father reading them when he does business in other countries. He and his aides go over every list carefully to see they are given everything on that list.

"There are twenty-two letters you must learn to write on your tablet and to recognize when you see them."

Jezebel heaved a sigh, leaned her clay tablet on the table to steady it, and began to draw each character several times.

"You must draw each one precisely as you see it on my tablet."

She squinted her eyes, gripped the stylus with determination and began to carve into the soft clay. She tried different ways to hold it steady so the lines would be straight. The curved lines were more difficult to manage. Haman helped her find a grip that would allow her to hold it steady and to see her work at the same time.

"Do other countries have these letters, too?"

"Yes. Most of them have their own. They like ours best because all the countries your father visits use ours. With the same letters he can do business wherever he goes."

"How do these look, Haman?"

"Quite good actually! Soon you will be able to read them and the words they make when you put them together."

Jezebel loved to please Haman, so she worked diligently for the next several weeks learning to draw them precisely and name them. Then he taught her to make words that represented something, like wine, oil, and spices.

Now fascinated, she was determined to master this by the time she went traveling with her father. She wrote and repeated the words over and over.

"Oh Haman, I want to read everything that is written! I want to know what those notes and lists say. My father will be proud of me when he takes me with him. I can go the market places and read the signs on the vendors' booths!"

"You must be patient and cautious, Jezebel. You are eager and often impulsive. That will get you into trouble and put you in danger. It would be wise if you kept your ability to read a secret until it is necessary for you to use it. Otherwise you will not be allowed to attend any meetings and not trusted. There is much competition in the business of trading and you do not want to be a liability for your father. These things I tell you are very important. Do you understand?"

Jezebel was much sobered by this. She had not heard Haman be so serious before.

"I do not understand! What danger would I possibly be in? I will be with my father."

"I know you want to enjoy your time and see new things at different ports, but ports draw bad people. They are looking to steal from the merchants. They abduct young girls to sell in the slave market.

"Do not go anywhere alone and if you see wrong doing, you must never let the person know you have seen them. Only tell your father about it when you are alone together."

"You are scaring me. Do you wish me to be afraid? I have never been afraid!"

"Jezebel, you are safe and well protected here. You can go about as you please. But in foreign ports you are not free to go about alone or wander through the markets without your guards. You have made a game of escaping from your guards here, but you must never do that away from the palace."

Jezebel put on her best pout and stamped her feet.

"How do you know? You have been spying on me, Haman!"

"Everyone here knows everything you do, Jezebel. Nothing you do is hidden. They let you believe you have escaped their notice, but you have not. They play your games because you have been a child, but now you must no longer do childish things.

"You are nearly twelve years old and you must mature in your thoughts and actions. It is good to begin acting as a wise adult and earn the respect you want."

Jezebel's world of make believe was shattered. No one had ever dared to criticize or correct her.

"I will tell my father you have not treated me with respect! I will tell him you are trying to make me afraid. I will tell him…"

Chapter 2

"Jezebel, your father has hired me to educate you and guide you in most every facet of life, not just entertain you with stories and teach you letters. Your childhood is passing away and you must begin to grow up into a wise and capable woman, one who can own property, govern a territory, and conduct trade with other countries."

Tears started running down her cheeks. Jezebel turned abruptly and stomped off to her spacious private rooms. She grabbed up a beautiful covering from the foot of her bed, wrapped it around her and cried angry tears into the brocaded flowers.

Her brother Eser, two years younger, came into her room and flopped down on the bed beside her.

"What are you crying about? Do you not know you will be a queen? And I will be a king. We will rule our world! We will not cry like children. Stop it, Jezebel!"

"But everyone has been spying on me! Laughing at me because they think I am a child. Well maybe I am, but they will not laugh at me anymore. I will show them!"

"You will show them what? How angry and mean you can be? Why not show them how calm and powerful you can be? That is how everyone wants you to be as a future Queen."

"How do you know?"

"I just know. Come on, Jezebel, smile while we walk to the dining hall together like the king and queen we are destined to be."

Eser, though two years younger, had a quiet sense of maturity. He was solidly built like his father and his eyes crinkled in the corners that suggested a smile. He was a favorite of the servants and the court. He was studious and could provide helpful information at any given time.

Jezebel got up, dried her tears, and looked into the tall mirror on the opposite wall. She briefly arranged her hair, lifted her chin, and turned to Eser over her shoulder flashing her brightest smile.

Eser got off the bed, bowed deeply and gave her his arm. Together they paraded in their most royal style, chins up and smiling, down the ornate halls to where the table boards were filled with delicious foods, beautiful table covers and flowers.

King Ethbaal and his entourage greeted them with smiles and blessings of Astarte. Then he turned to Jezebel and she knew what was coming. He was the only one who could chastise her. She knew she must listen and be respectful.

"You are doing well in your studies, Jezebel! Haman tells me you are working hard and accomplishing more than Eser, here. But then Eser is younger and will catch up in no time."

Eser wanted to protest that he was doing well, too, but knew not to say anything. He kept quiet, chin up, and did not smile or frown. Ethbaal turned a kindly eye to Eser and put his hand on Eser's shoulder.

"I know you want to protest, Eser, but I know you will not, because you have learned a lesson Jezebel has yet to master."

"What lesson, Father? I have heard everything Haman has said to me."

"Yes, you heard it, but you became angry and ran off to your rooms in tears like a child. This must not happen ever again. Every lesson is a blessing, every criticism is a blessing. We learn from both. But you learn nothing if you react like a child. Do you understand, Jezebel?"

"Yes, Father."

Jezebel was subdued and ready to burst into tears again. She desperately wanted to run to her rooms, but knew she must not. She held her breath and willed herself to be still and not cry.

"Now, Jezebel, remember I love you and am proud of you. I want to take you on the ship with me. I must be sure you know who you are and how you must act in a grown up way. So please, now let us consider the lesson learned and enjoy our meal."

Jezebel swallowed hard, let her breath out slowly, and managed a smile. Eser kicked her under the table. She wanted to kick him back harder, but she just smiled at him.

"I will practice on you, my dear brother."

"And I will practice on you, my dear sister."

All the adults at the meal began chatting with each other to Jezebel's relief. This was not the kind of attention she wanted. She wanted to be admired and she was determined to earn admiration, respect, and even fealty.

She would not give Eser the chance to surpass her again. She kicked him back under the table, smiled at him, and began to reach for the food. She was famished.

Sidon was a city state ruled by King Ethbaal. Tyre was a city state ruled by King Phelles and his three brothers before him. Competition in trade was ruthless among the municipalities along the coast of the Great Sea, especially between Sidon and Tyre. Sidon was losing the competition. It was becoming poorer while Tyre was becoming richer and more powerful. Ethbaal needed Tyre and eventually Carthage to increase his territory and power. Tyre and King Phelles were standing in the way.

There were many difficulties in Tyre. Brigands sent by King Phelles would vandalize Ethbaal's ships and murder his crew members. His merchant bins would be filled with sand instead of the goods Ethbaal purchased on the Tyre trading floor.

There was only one way to end the theft and murders of his crew. He sent his spies to assassinate King Phelles of Tyre. This was not difficult since King Phelles was so sure of his power he often walked the torch lit docks at night without a guard.

Ethbaal rejoiced at the news the assassination was successful. Now he could take over Tyre and expand his kingdom to include all of Phoenicia and beyond. Ethbaal was thirty six when he created his new dynasty. He was a big man with a full luxurious beard and moustache. His bearing was kingly even though he was not overly tall. He would reign thirty two years as priest of Astarte and King of Tyre now that his rival, King Phelles, was gone.

King Ethbaal's merchant ships backed away from the loading docks and turned out into the bay of Sidon. Loaded with glass for which Sidon was famous, jewelry, artwork, perfume, wool, linen textile and olive oil. They would stop at Tyre for the royal purple dyes and other goods. They then traveled along the coast stopping at all the ports from Tyre to Rhacotis.

Jezebel and Eser stood together on the bow and let the wind whip their hair and robes as they sailed away. Now the whole of Phoenicia belonged to them as children of King Ethbaal. It was safer for them to travel with him.

In the beginning Haman kept them diligent in learning the arts of negotiation, marketing, record keeping, and even sailing. Eser was fascinated with everything. Jezebel yawned from time to time, especially when it came to record keeping.

"Soon we will be docking at Gaza. We can see the port over there!"

Eser was thrilled but Jezebel was a little disappointed. It did not look like much from far away. As they got closer she could see the docks were busy and crates were piled up everywhere.

Eser was already helping to bring the ship into the berth. Jezebel was ready to jump off onto the dock.

"Do not go without me, Jezebel. We have to stay together so nothing will happen to you."

"You worry so much! Nothing will happen to me. Hurry up! We must get to the market place before everyone else does. The best purchases are the early ones before everything is picked over and the squabbling over prices begins."

"But Father has already bought the goods and they are being loaded as soon as other cargo is unloaded for the merchants who ordered them. I have the list right here."

She looked with disgust at the records he was holding.

"Just look at it, Jezebel, it is not difficult."

"Well, it is boring. I prefer negotiating in the market places. It is fun to bargain the merchants down to almost nothing."

"Remember, Jezebel, if you destroy their profits they will not trade with you. At least pretend to be fair. We must protect our suppliers and see to their success, too."

"That sounds weak, like nonsense. I will ask Haman tomorrow. He will know better than you."

"Haman is an old man. Do not lean on him too hard. He may crumble and turn to dust."

Incensed, Jezebel hurried down the dock to the market stalls to survey the jewelry and silk scarves. She loved to imagine herself as a Queen wearing them. She selected what she wanted and called one of their sailors to pick them up and pay the merchant.

Eser was close by. He hated having to run after the impetuous Jezebel, but he could see no alternative. He knew she would need him.

Chapter 3

"Where are we going next? I want to leave as soon as possible." Eser's patience was wearing thin. It seemed she was purposely provoking him, pushing and trying to control everything.

"You are not yet a queen, Jezebel. Please follow me and stay close. We are going to the Temple of Dagon to honor Baal's father as our father has commanded us to do."

She heaved a sigh.

"Lead on, my princely brother. I am at your command."

There was no mistaking the location of the Temple of Dagon. It was enormous. The statue of Dagon was like a giant looking out over the Great Sea. It had huge bulging eyes and great hands full of offerings of grain.

"See, here are smaller statues around the Temple of Dagon. These are frescoes of him as a fish blessing the fishermen with abundant catches to feed and prosper everyone."

Jezebel turned up her nose.

"I prefer the Temple of Astarte. She is beautiful and I love to cover her altars with flowers and fruit. She is the sister of Dagon's consort, Ishara, you know. I just prefer the female gods who are so beautiful, not ugly like Dagon."

A priest of Dagon came out from behind a huge pillar and confronted Jezebel.

"Be careful of what you say, Princess. The gods can hear and will make you suffer for your disrespect!"

Jezebel flashed her loveliest smile at the priest and bowed with folded hands.

"Of course. I do beg Dagon's pardon. Does Dagon pardon or forgive? Astarte does."

Eser dropped an offering at the feet of Dagon, took Jezebel's arm, guided her out of the temple, and back toward the docks.

"One day your lack of wisdom and decorum will get you killed, Jezebel."

"Ah, but you are always here to rescue me, are you not? You enjoy rescuing me. Does that not make you feel powerful and strong?"

"I am powerful and strong, and you are spoiled and willful. You think everything will always go your way. Someday it may not."

The oarlocks groaned as the oarsmen pushed the ship away from the dock, turned it into the bay, and out to sea. Rhacotis was the next stop and the winds were favorable. The sails flapped in the wind and then snapped into place when the sailors anchored them.

Eser was in a small cabin writing an inventory of what was in the ship's hold as they headed for Rhacotis. Jezebel reluctantly agreed to help him. They matched the contracts with goods supposed to be on board and fortunately their records matched what was on the ship.

"What makes this so important that we must spend time matching the record with what we have? Will we not know when we get home if there is a shortage?"

"Yes, we will, but it will be too late. We will not know where the shortage happened. You can go to the markets and souks and bargain for small purchases. It cannot be that way for shiploads."

"Why not, Eser? How is it done?"

"Our father has professional trades people in the Trading Center of Tyre who negotiate the prices and arrange everything with other negotiators before we even load the ships. It is that very agreement we are looking at together. The work has been done for us. The trading is already done.

"But we must make sure what is in this agreement is done on the docks. If we check it after visiting each city, we will know which city caused a shortage and someone will come from Tyre to that city and see it is made right."

"You are two years younger than I am, and yet how do you know so much about these things!"

"I listen to the traders and sometimes go to the Trading Center in Tyre to learn more. Jezebel, you must learn these things too. You will find they are much more fascinating than a few transactions for silks at a market.

"Promise you will come with me and we will learn them together. I will be a king and you a queen, but there is no difference in what we must know in order to rule."

"Somehow I thought all of this would be men's work."

"That is what someone might hope you would think. You must not let it keep you from being as educated and smart as you can! You cannot trust anyone to know these things for you. It would keep you in a weakened position. If you are to be powerful, you must know all you can."

Jezebel thought about it as they began the voyage toward Rhacotis. She began to have a different feeling about herself and who she must become. Now the excitement permeated her whole being.

All day she sat with Eser and the records. She learned to keep her own records to double check with his. When they reached Rhacotis in the afternoon a few days later she did not go to the markets.

She went to the offices on the docks with Eser. She identified the cargo with what was on her record. As always with Jezebel, when she was interested she would comprehend the information in a short time and become an expert.

"We will be in Rhacotis for a few days, so let us find a suitable inn in which to lodge and rest. You can go to the market if you want to. I will be happy to go with you. You can teach me about silks, jewels, and other things."

Jezebel smiled a bright happy smile at him.

"You will go with me? I would love it!"

Eser was amazed. This was no longer his petulant sister, but a true partner on the path. Eagerly they awaited the docking at Rhacotis and left the ship to find an inn. One was pointed out to them by their captain who knew which ones were safe. They were owned by Phoenicians who would guard them discretely.

"Prince Eser and Princess Jezebel! We are most honored you have chosen my establishment. I am the owner and your humble servant, Ahinadab of Tyre. My staff will see to whatever you need for your comfort."

Two servants approached, bowed, and guided them to their rooms.

"These rooms look so different. The images and decorations are strange to me."

"We are in Egypt, Jezebel. Is it not wonderful? I love Egyptian art.

"But they do they really worship a bird!"

"They have hundreds of gods to represent every aspect of their lives, harvests and animals. There are many farmers in our land keeping little statues of gods in their homes to insure good weather and harvests, but we know Baal and Astarte are over them all.

"But in Canaan, I am told the statues look like people, not birds."

"My favorite Egyptian is Pharaoh Akhenaten who believed the sun was god and had an image of himself created with the Sun-Disc over his head. It is thought the Hebrew, Moses, brought the belief in one god from Egypt and created the religion of the Jews."

"Where did you learn this?"

"The Egyptians draw pictures instead of making words with letter characters. It is easy to read their pictures, but not efficient for making trading records on clay tablets. Our letters have been adopted by the merchants at the Port of Rhacotis so they can trade with us.

"Egypt is much larger with many villages and different people living along the river past the great pyramids. Pictures are easier for them to understand."

Famished, they went down to the dining room for a meal and continued the conversation.

"You must tell me all you know about Egypt! Why have you not told me about this before?"

"Jezebel, you would not listen. You were not interested! But now you are, so I will be happy to tell you what little I know."

Chapter 4

Jezebel and Eser finished their meal and got up from the table to leave. When they turned toward the door a tall man in royal vestments stood in the doorway. Ahinadab rushed to introduce the Prince of Egypt, Prince Seti, and bowed deeply in acknowledgment of his royal highness.

He was handsome and charming. Jezebel began to regret just coming off the ship without her normal careful grooming. He was looking at her and she could not take her eyes away from him. He politely turned to Eser.

"You are Baal Eser II, son of King Ethbaal, and you must be the beautiful Princess Jezebel, daughter of the king. Welcome to my country!"

Jezebel gathered her wits and smiled her most sparkling smile. She bowed briefly as befits a princess. He took her hand and gently brushed his lips across it. A thrill ran through her whole body like she had never experienced in her life.

"Please, be my guest while you are here and allow me to show you the wonders of Egypt. My chariot is just outside."

"A chariot? I have never seen one."

The prince offered Jezebel his arm and escorted her out to his gold guilt chariot and prancing black Arabian horses. Surprised and confused, Eser hesitated and glanced at Ahinadab. Ahinadab smiled bleakly and gestured toward the door.

"Thank you for your kind welcome. We will return."

A little embarrassed and hoping Prince Seti would not leave him behind, he strode out into the bright sun and followed them.

"You have not ridden in a chariot before, my dear. Here is where you step up and this bar is where you hang on. I will ride behind both of you to keep you safe because chariots are a bumpy ride, even on smooth roads."

Seti lifted Jezebel up into the chariot. Eser climbed in just behind her. He was becoming quite distrusting of this smooth talking Egyptian prince. He was too easy and familiar, especially with his sister.

Should he not be more reserved as befits royalty? Jezebel and I are also royalty and Seti should respect that.

Seti hopped up onto the chariot, picked up the reins and snapped them on the horses' backs. The horses leaped into action straining against the harnesses of the extra heavy chariot. They pulled it forward with a lurch nearly causing Jezebel and Eser to lose their footing.

Seti put his arm around Jezebel to steady her, while Eser grabbed for the hand rail that went around the front and sides. It caused Eser to feel embarrassed and angry at the same time.

As Jezebel regained her normal composure, she became her vibrant snappy self. She conversed with Seti easily, responding to his humor, and tossing her hair in the breeze as they rode along.

"Where are we going?"

"I want to show you our palace, the Great River, Iteru, that brings the harvests, and the great pyramids at Kher Neter. The pyramids are the burial places of the great pharaohs, Khufu, Khafre, and Menikaure. Iteru, the Great River, flows four thousand miles to empty into the Great Sea right there at Rhacotis."

"How far are we going? The day is half spent. We should be back at the inn by this evening."

"It is many miles, but the road is good. We will stop at an inn and continue the rest of the way early in the morning. It is worth the distance and time to see the pyramids and the sphinxes that symbolically guard them."

Seti was turned toward her and his back was to Eser. She began to feel cornered and was not about to let this go on. Her haughty demeanor returned and she rounded on him.

"We did not plan for an extra night of travel. This is most inconvenient."

"All will be provided for your comfort at the inn. Please do not be concerned."

"I hope you intend to include Eser in our conversations, Prince Seti. He will soon be a king and it would be wise for you to establish favor with him."

"But of course!"

Somewhat chastened, Seti moved the horses along a little faster now that the road was smooth enough.

Eser took a deep breath of relief although he was not happy about this turn of events. But now he was sure Jezebel was not being taken in by this smooth talking, overbearing prince. She could stand on her own and command the respect her royalty required.

Jezebel and Eser were astonished at the sheer size of the pyramids. Eser stepped out of the chariot to examine the huge stones and to marvel at the height of the building rising into the bright blue sky. He walked to the entrance of the closest one, which was blocked.

Seti dutifully accompanied him and walked behind him. Jezebel was admiring the huge sphinxes.

"All of this to bury one man?"

"Yes, and all of his worldly wealth so he can live as a god in the next life. There are many hallways in the pyramid the workers used to access the great rooms to paint the frescoes depicting the life and victories of the Pharaoh.

"Upon completion, those walkways were blocked and the builders were all sealed inside. This was to prevent grave robbers from bribing or torturing them to learn the true way to the Pharaoh's sarcophagus and his wealth, thereby disturbing his eternal life."

"You killed them all?"

"It was necessary. They knew that when they agreed to plan the building."

Eser wondered if they signed on willingly. He doubted it. They went to the palace for a short visit and a brief meal. Eser stayed close to Jezebel as they looked at the enormous open air rooms and columns.

They saw nothing they liked in the cold interior or anything about Seti that gave them peace of mind. It was a relief to be traveling back to Rhacotis in a carriage in the morning and in time for the evening meal at Ahinadab's inn.

"I must apologize I did not have the carriage yesterday. I always travel in the chariot. I did not know you were here until I arrived in Rhacotis on business. I did not want to miss the opportunity of a visit with you and give you a tour of a small but important part of Egypt."

Eser knew he was trying to smooth things with Jezebel on the way back to the city, and he had no business in Rhacotis because princes would not do business on their own.

Jezebel was not to be placated by this man. The more he talked the more incensed she became.

"Prince Seti, my brother Eser and I are here on business as you know from our ships moored in the harbor. However, the actual business is done by professional trade negotiators in Tyre, not by royalty. So I cannot imagine what business you would be doing in Rhacotis."

Stunned, Seti sat back in the carriage seat and folded his hands in his lap. He looked from Jezebel to Eser and back to Jezebel.

"You are perceptive, Jezebel. The truth is our government institutions have broken down over the last two hundred years. The office of prince has only a bloodline to establish it, but no power and little royal privilege. The best I can do is come here to watch the business transactions, see where the money is flowing, and advise those in power.

"Of course they do not value what I tell them. They are not interested in the good of Egypt, only the riches they can amass and servant girls to do their every bidding. Only by marrying into royalty from another land could I regain some of the prestige, but without the prestige here in Egypt first, it is not likely to happen."

Eser and Jezebel sat silent for a long time, not sure how to respond. This was a different Seti than the one who had swept them away from Rhacotis the day before.

"I hope I have not embarrassed you. I usually do not lay bare all of the disappointments of my position. In fact I have never done this. It is most unprincely, I am sure. But somehow your genuineness and honesty brought it out of me. You are the first honest people I have encountered. I do not know what to say from here except to wish you the best of good fortune. You are a credit to Phoenicia and all it stands for."

They arrived in Rhacotis and went to Ahinadab's inn for rest and a late evening meal. Seti declined their invitation to join them, saying he must return to the palace. He bid them farewell with thanks for their kindness. Jezebel and Eser bowed royal to royal, as did Seti and kissing Jezebel's hand he departed.

Jezebel and Eser spent what remained of the evening and part of the night going over the cargo count, seeing all was in order for their journey home.

"I am proud of you, Jezebel. I know I will not have to worry about protecting you. You are quite capable of taking care of yourself, and me for that matter. You know who you are. I know nothing will defeat you. You see what is happening around you and know what to do."

"I am proud of you, too, my dear brother! You have a quiet power and wisdom that befits a king. And may I say, I love you and care about you. I will always be here for you."

Before dawn the loading of the ship was well under way. Eser and Jezebel boarded and settled themselves for the journey. The rowers backed the ship away from the dock and turned toward the east and Gaza as the sails went up.

The ship docked in Gaza for the night and continued to Tyre and Sidon in the morning. Two different people from the way they were at the start of the trip now stood together on the bow of the ship. They talked over the successful journey, an interesting encounter with a prince who revealed the stagnating condition of Egypt, and what events they might look forward to as they arrived home.

Chapter 5

The ship docked a few hours late due to unfavorable winds that came up suddenly. The trip was a little rough. Jezebel and Eser were happy to see the harbor at last. King Ethbaal anxiously awaited the return of his children. Even though they were maturing and enjoying the privilege and protection of royalty, he could not help but worry about them when they were far away.

The king's council gathered in the great hall to hear the reports of the latest journey. Ethbaal, Jezebel, Eser, the ship's captain, the primary negotiator, several advisors to the king, and Haman were present. Each one gave their report. Then it came to Jezebel and Eser.

Eser usually gave the report, boosting his father's pride in him. This time it was Jezebel giving their report with Eser assisting. It was clear to all the two had become a team and worked well together.

Haman's old eyes were beaming with pride. He had done his job well and these two were the proof. He was aging and becoming frail, leaning more heavily on his walking stick. He was no longer their teacher but his purpose now was to always be their friend.

Eser and Jezebel decided they should go to the Trading Center in Tyre to learn what they could. These were the experts who created trade agreements, set prices, and communicated what goods would be put on ships and sent to other ports.

"It sounds exciting! Do you think they will allow us to visit the trading floor?"

"I have been there. I was not allowed down on the floor itself, because it might interrupt the bidding and trading, so I was given reports instead."

"That is disappointing. Could you see the traders and what they do?"

"Only from a distance, but it was still exciting and noisy because when they bid, they shout at each other. And they run back and forth conferring with each other. Let me get the reports they gave me and we will look at them together before we go."

The reports were indecipherable except for a few city names and other words. Jezebel was puzzled trying to read them.

"They use codes and we do not know what they mean. Maybe Haman could help us. He knows so much. More than you seem to think, Eser."

"I do regret the remark I made about Haman while we were in Gaza. I was frustrated."

"Probably my fault too. I was pushing and demanding. Forgive me."

Haman was in his quarters studying artifacts he had brought from his travels in other countries. He kept a list of them, where they were from, and what they represented.

"Come in my children. How good to see you! What brings you here on this lovely day? What have you there?"

Jezebel and Eser were not children, but they knew it was a term of endearment and smiled. Eser handed him the reports from the Trading Center.

He looked the sheets up and down in surprise, holding them close so his aging eyes could see them.

"Ah, I have not seen one of these for many years. What do you want to know?"

"Haman, we are planning to go to the Trading Center in Tyre and hoped you could help us understand these codes and symbols."

"Jezebel, you are always so curious and that is good! Let me see, now..."

Jezebel and Eser leaned in close as Haman pointed with an aged crooked finger to rows of marks and symbols.

"This column is the city the goods are coming from. This one is the city they are going to. The next column is symbols for what they are and how many. At the bottom is the price paid for the incoming and the price to be received for those about to be shipped out.

"There are different reports for the caravans that go across the land to different countries. Everything is carefully noted every day for every ship and caravan. The symbols make it easier. Everyone knows what they mean, and they take up little space in the report. Otherwise you would have many, many pages."

"I want to know what the symbols mean. Where can I find their meanings?"

"Jezebel, there are hundreds of them, different for every country and every kind of goods. Let us begin with symbols for our own goods sold to our ports around the Great Sea."

"I will, but then I want to know them all!"

Eser sat quietly by smiling and knowing Jezebel would get what she wanted and he would share in it.

"I will bring you a man who is retired from trading and very crippled. If he is well enough to come here, he can help you begin."

Jezebel was content for the moment, but Eser was thinking ahead.

"We will delay our visit to the Trading Center in Tyre until we understand more. Then when we go, we will know what is being done. We will tell no one we have this knowledge. We will use it to watch over our country's trading, as we did on the ship."

Jezebel and Eser went to King Ethbaal that evening to explain their plans and he was amazed.

"Yes, of course and you will have whatever you need. I am sure Haman will bring you the best teacher. My libraries will provide what he needs to educate you. Our country will be safer and more efficient if you know the deep workings of its trade."

Philosir turned out to be a wonderful teacher. His body was so crippled that he could not do much else. A servant carried him into the library, laid him down on a chaise, and wrapped him in a thick quilt.

At first the study of the symbols was daunting, but Philosir was patient, explaining that the symbols had a pattern to them. He showed them how they were clustered with similar meanings and how they branched out from the basics as trade demanded.

Jezebel and Eser kept a rigorous study schedule and tested each other with mock trading exercises and games. How the traders could use the patterns to create prices and quantities became more and more understandable as they studied.

"Come, Jezebel, we must go to the docks and test our skill there. I remember seeing the symbols on the documents you and I studied on the ship. They are also written on the bundles and crates. Surely we can learn more there and ask Philosir about anything we do not understand."

They set out early the next morning for the docks before their lesson in the afternoon with Philosir. They had gone through many bundles and piles of goods all along the dock when a guard shouted at them and came running toward them.

"Who are you? What are you doing?"

They were shocked and stood up. Eser was quick with a confident answer.

"We are working for King Ethbaal who has allowed us to inspect the shipments."

"You will come with me and we will see about that!"

He took each of them by the arm and pushed them toward a small building on the dock. The building was rough and smelly. Inside they were seated on the greasy floor. Jezebel became angrier by the minute.

A message was sent to the captain of the king's guards that spies or thieves had been caught on the docks.

"Where did you get these fine clothes? Did you steal them out of one of the bundles waiting to be loaded onto a ship?"

Jezebel roared up off the floor and looked the guard in the eye.

"I am Princess Jezebel and this is my brother Prince Baal-Eser II and we have stolen nothing!"

The guard was about to laugh in her face when Haman came in the door of the building pounding his walking stick on the floor. A guard from the palace of King Ethbaal came in with him.

"A mistake has been made here. These are indeed the children of King Ethbaal, entrusted to learn the ways of trade and marketing. A message was sent to you, but it must not have arrived."

The dock guard bowed and mumbled his apologies.

"No need to apologize for doing your job well. Nothing more will be said of this. Please continue on with your work."

Chapter 6

The four walked down the dock toward shore.

"I have a carriage waiting to take us back. I am too old and lame to walk all the way down here and back. It would be good if you two would make arrangements for a visit like this for your safety and the safety of that poor rattled dock guard! However, you did prove the guard is vigilant and efficient. That is good to know."

Jezebel reverted to her childhood fears that Haman would reprimand her but he did not. Relieved she would own her part with a mature response.

"Also it is good for us to know we should remember our responsibility to be more thoughtful and to do what is wise. How did you know we were there?"

"The walls have ears, Jezebel. The wall have ears. Now, what did you learn?"

Yes, she remembered nothing she did was secret. Everyone in the palace knew everything she did.

"Mostly where the symbols and numbers are stamped on the crates of goods. That is all we came there to do and then the guard arrested us. Imagine, he thought we were thieves!"

"How did you like being in his guard building?"

Jezebel wrinkled her nose.

"It was dirty and smelled bad. But that is true of most things on a seaport dock. Dead fish, animal dung and who knows what else."

Eser climbed into the carriage after helping Jezebel and Haman up the step.

"And we will have appropriate documents in hand."

"Thank you, Eser. I was hoping one of you would mention it. Even though you are both royalty, you must still have official identification wherever you go, and have it on your person, not left behind in a bundle at a hotel."

The noise of the Trading Center could be heard from quite a distance as Eser and Jezebel approached by carriage. The Trading Center looked larger and larger the closer they got. It was covered with a huge white tent over two stories high.

Jezebel and Eser walked in cautiously. Immediately they were met and escorted by a door guard to a gallery area off to the side.

The floors inside were covered with marble slabs which had colorful paintings of ships and caravans on each slab. Tables and benches where scattered around the edge where clerks were seated. Higher up on platforms were the investors overseeing the trading, signaling their negotiators with gestures.

The clerks were shouting and negotiators dashing everywhere. It looked incredibly chaotic and exciting! They watched with fascination. Despite their recent studies of the symbols and ways of making trades, they had a difficult time sorting out who was doing what.

They sat in the gallery until evening came and the trading ceased at the blast of a horn. Everyone exited the building immediately. Suddenly it was empty and quiet. The guard came to Eser and indicated they should come with him.

Outside, Jezebel turned to the guard.

"Is there no hospitality here? We came from Sidon!"

"Yes, Your Highness. King Ethbaal has taken care of everything. There is an inn not far down the road. We hope you will find it to your satisfaction. Your driver has been notified of the location. They are expecting you."

She sniffed and walked to the carriage. Eser smiled. Jezebel just could not let go of the haughty edge in her voice when speaking to uppity servants and others not of her high rank.

The inn was beautiful and accommodating. As befits the welcoming of royalty, the servants were lined up outside to greet them along with the innkeeper. Inside a meal was prepared and about to be served.

The wine was poured as they stepped in the door. They were escorted to their places at a small banquet table surrounded by gauzy flowing curtains in a quiet area of the dining room. There were vases of fresh flowers set around and music being played on a small harp. More flowing draperies separated them from the other guests.

Jezebel was ready for another adventure.

"Haman mentioned caravans. Where do the caravans go? When do they leave and come back? Can we travel with them?"

"Right now I must follow our father into the priesthood of Astarte and you will go to Byblos to study The Lady of Byblos, Baalat Gubal. She is a sister of Astarte, Anat, Isis, and Hathor. You will like the Egyptian influences in Byblos. Maybe you will find a real prince there. Egypt is dead in the land of Egypt, but alive in Byblos."

"I do not need a prince, real or not! How do you know all this, little brother?"

"Haman the tutor. I was sure father would send us away for religious education soon, so I asked Haman."

Once again, Eser was ahead of Jezebel. If she did not love him so much she would hate him. He and Haman were her best and most trusted friends. How could she not love them? But still her goal was to excel in all she did and it meant staying ahead of Eser. This was her measure of how she was accomplishing it.

King Ethbaal requested Eser and Jezebel come to speak with him in his meeting room. Eser was sure it would be instructions for their training as priest and priestess. Jezebel did not believe it would happen. Surely she would not be sent away!

"Jezebel we have a ship going to Byblos soon and you can sail there to start your training in the school to be a priestess of Astarte. The training will be one year and you must do well."

"Must I leave here for a whole year? Why so long, and why would I not do well?"

"Because, my dear daughter, the training is about spiritual power, obedience, love, and humility. Those are the necessary virtues you must have to please Astarte and to be her priestess. They are not learned in a week or two. They are to become your way of life. You must represent Astarte wherever you are throughout your life. It is expected of you as a Phoenician royal princess."

Jezebel was floored. He was really sending her away!

"This sounds like punishment! Have I done something to displease you, my father?"

"No, Jezebel. Just the opposite. You have excelled in everything you take on and I am proud of you. But there are necessary virtues you must learn that have not been included in your training up until now. This training will protect you with Astarte's love. It will bring you spiritual power that is not about earthly things."

"When must I go?"

"The ship is being prepared and loaded tonight. You will leave early in the morning as soon as it is dawn and the tide is right. There will be two guards who will accompany you and be close by at all times. They are Hannibal and Barek. Byblos has a diverse population with many religions and cultures. Please respect that I have sent them to guard you wherever you travel."

"Thank you, my father. I will come to understand all of this in time, I am sure."

King Ethbaal laughed a hearty laugh.

"I am sure you will fight it like a mother tiger protecting her cubs! Go now with my blessing. Remember to enjoy your life there and wherever you are."

Enjoy her life? Jezebel felt like her life had just been wrenched from her and turned upside down. She wanted to cry and throw a tantrum, but knew she did not dare. She kissed her father's cheek, bowed deeply, and walked away as gracefully as she could.

She wanted to run as fast and as far as her legs would carry her, but she did not give in to the impulse. When she calmed down, she would go to find her dear friend and tutor, Haman. He would help her steady herself and know how to go forward into the next part of her education.

Enjoy my life? I will die! Just die!"

Chapter 7

The ship had just cleared the breakwater and slipped into a berth at the dock in Byblos. Her guards wanted her to wait while they cleared the dock of people so she could safely get to her waiting carriage.

"You will not clear the dock and I will not wait here! I have been everywhere on voyages and travels without your help. Just stay out of my way!"

She pushed past the guards and headed for the gang plank. On the dock no one recognized her or cared who she was. Everyone went about their business which gave Jezebel the opportunity to stop and take in the scene around her.

To her surprise there were Egyptian ships unloading and loading, and Egyptian sailors everywhere. This was not her experience of Egypt in Rhacotis. This looked like a prosperous Egypt. *Did the prince lie to me about conditions there?*

She walked past the waiting carriage and onto the streets. There were indeed people from other places. Strange dress, goods she had difficulty recognizing, and several different languages bursting forth all around her. The guards trotted along behind her, frustrated and confused as to what they should do.

"Jezebel! Princess Jezebel, is that you?"

She turned toward the voice to see an astonished Prince Seti standing there.

"Yes, of course I am Princess Jezebel. Seti! What are you doing here? Why are all these Egyptian ships here? Has Egypt completely collapsed and everyone is escaping to Byblos?"

Seti burst out laughing.

"Now I am sure you are Jezebel! Who else would confront a prince of Egypt in such a manner? What are you doing here? We must find an inn to sit and talk."

"I am on my way to the School of Astarte and my guards are about to grab you and haul you away."

"Guards? You have guards. Where?"

"Behind you. They are here at my father's insistence."

She motioned for them to come forward.

"These are Hannibal and Barek, my guards while I am in Byblos. I am told it is a dangerous city."

Seti greeted them politely but they did not respond.

"It is a dangerous city, but exciting too. You will not need guards while you are with me. I am known here."

"Oh, how lovely! I am sure my father will disapprove of my being with someone he does not know. Until the guards get further orders from King Ethbaal, they will stay on duty and no assurances from you will change that."

Jezebel walked toward her guards and signaled they should take her to the School of Astarte. They escorted her to the carriage much relieved.

Seti was disappointed as he watched the carriage disappear into the tangle of city streets. He thought about Jezebel many times since their first meeting but did not expect to see her again. Now another chance to be with her had slipped away from him as suddenly as it arrived.

Upon entering the ornate gate of the school, a tall woman in flowing robes, with a graceful walk approach her. She had shining hair, skin, and eyes that seemed to radiate light.

"Welcome Princess Jezebel! We have been expecting you. Your rooms are ready. Our priestesses guided your guards to where your baggage should be placed and all is in order.

"I am High Priestess Manot and I will show you around. Please come with me."

The High Priestess walked away fully expecting Jezebel to follow. Jezebel was a little irritated at this brief welcome but quietly obeyed the High Priestess.

They walked through huge halls and beautiful rooms. Everything was brightly painted with frescoes of Astarte's power and love. There were symbols from several different cultures, some seemed to be Egyptian. The floors were gold and pink marble. There were flowing curtains in the doorways and vases of flowers everywhere.

The fragrance of the sea and smells of the docks were soon forgotten amid the flowers and their sweet perfumes. Jezebel had seen other palaces, but none were as lovely as this place. She could not help but feel softened by the atmosphere. Her initial irritation was slipping away.

"Our Astarte is also known as the Lady of Byblos, Baalat Gubal, Anat, Isis, and Hathor, depending upon who is speaking of her and what culture the person is from."

"Please, High Priestess, tell me what I am to expect from the teachings and what the classes are like. I have never been in a classroom with other students, only with my tutor. Sometimes I am joined by my brother. Here, I am at a loss."

"A companion and friend is assigned to be at your side. She will guide you through the lessons and all you need to accomplish. Her name is Ashara and you will meet her shortly."

"I have never had a woman friend. Is she like a servant?"

"No, she is not a servant. We do not have servants here. The priestesses in training do all that needs to be done and it is their joy to serve. They rotate tasks every month so they can learn many things and be educated in all realms."

"And will I be expected to do these tasks as well? I am a royal princess, you know."

"Yes, I know. But here we are all equal in the eyes of Astarte. We are sisters and friends. Even after you complete your training and choose to leave, they will always hold you in their hearts and prayers forever."

Jezebel could feel her anger and impatience rising again and she tried to fight it down. There were no choices offered except to follow along.

She paused, took a deep breath, and focused on this lovely High Priestess before her. *She is other-worldly, a goddess, and like a queen in more ways than I have ever seen anywhere.*

"But High Priestess, I have never been expected to do menial tasks. The life of a princess is different. She has servants who do all those things. I do not know what being equal means. No one is my equal in Phoenicia. My brother is to be the king and I will probably be married to a king for political gain for Phoenicia, or be in command of a city state. How can this training prepare me for those high offices?"

"I understand how puzzling this must be for you, Princess Jezebel. And I am sure your father, King Ethbaal, has your best interests in mind by sending you to us. Your training is his command and we will do our highest and best to fulfill it. Our ways are different, we know, and in time they will become more familiar and pleasing to you."

As they continued to walk, a young woman, diminutive in stature with a ready smile and dancing eyes met them. Her hair was a lustrous wavy dark brown and her eyes were dark as kohl.

"I am Ashara, Princess Jezebel. I am delighted to be chosen to be your friend and companion. We will be together through all of your training. Your name while you are here is Aishah. We will not refer to you as Jezebel. In our hearts you will always be Aishah now and beyond your training, throughout your life."

"How can my name be changed and for what reason?"

"In the presence of Astarte we leave references to our past behind and take on a new life. The new name represents the change."

"But I am Princess Jezebel! The world of Phoenicia knows me by that name!"

"Yes, we understand and now you are Aishah. You will come to know why you are given a new name as the training advances. It is important."

High Priestess Minot smiled at both of them.

"I will leave you two now. Dinner will soon be served. Before dinner the bells will ring and harp music will begin. You will go to the vesper chapel for devotions before dinner."

Jezebel wanted to round on Ashara about the name, but she looked into those trusting loving eyes and could not. She was completely disarmed.

"Come with me, Aishah. Trust that nothing will be taken from you, but only wonderful attributes added to you. Think of it as a most beautiful and exciting adventure that will empower you all of your life."

She took Aishah's hand and Jezebel reluctantly walked with Ashara to the vesper chapel. *Nothing will be taken from me. How can this be? Am I still a princess? Who is this Aishah and what is her part?*

Chapter 8

The bells were gentle and melodic. The harp music was beautiful and sweet. The chapel was decorated with an altar of flowers. The draperies flowed in the doorway in colors fading into each other.

High Priestess Minot began to recite the blessings of Astarte and all joined her in singing those blessings. Then they sat in silence for a period of time until the dinner was announced by music.

At dinner there was delicious food and merry laughter among the priestesses, but Aishah had no appetite for either. She felt uprooted, dazed, and disoriented. There was nothing here to emotionally anchor her, not even her own name.

"Come with me, Aishah. I will take you to our room we will share. Tunics, robes, and sandals will be laid out on the divans. They will be replaced fresh every day."

Aishah looked around at everything, laid down on a soft bed, and gave in immediately to exhaustion and sleep.

Ashara covered her with a light cover and lay down beside her. She prayed to Astarte for guidance in all the ways she would tutor and help Aishah.

Before dawn Aishah awakened to the gentle sound of the silver bells. She sat up and looked around but the room was dark. Ashara was immediately at her side.

"You are safe. You are at the School of Astarte, Aishah. Do you remember?"

Ashara lit a small lamp on a table nearby, put her arm around Aishah's shoulders and kissed her cheek.

"Oh, yes. Now I remember. How long have I slept? Is it still the middle of the night?"

"It is nearly dawn and the vesper bells are calling us to the chapel. Here, slip on this tunic, robe, and sandals. We will go together."

"Ashara, I have never been touched by a woman. I do not know how to understand what is meant by it. I have not even been touched by a man except for my brother who hit me from time to time, but he has not done that since he was a young boy."

"I am sure it may seem strange to you for a little while. We touch as a way of supporting each other's energy and wellbeing. I will tell you more about that today. Come, we must not be late."

Aishah tried to remember she was Princes Jezebel, but those thoughts were fleeting as they walked into the chapel. The music, quiet singing, and the fragrance of the flowers, overtook her attention. It was all so different than anything she had ever experienced and she could not help but enjoy it.

After they broke their fast they sat beneath a lovely arbor and Ashara began the lesson about touching and energy.

"I know touching royalty by commoners is forbidden and rightly so. It is for safety and protection, to keep people from grabbing at clothing and jewelry, and generally soiling or injuring the royal person. A distance shows respect.

"Here at Astarte's school and at the temples, it is a sign of devotion, support, and love. We have an energy within us that is always moving to keep us alive at all levels of being. Touching transfers our energy to each other and it is especially beneficial for those who are exhausted or not well. It is called a healing touch. No disrespect or sexual innuendo is implied or appropriate here."

"Is it required for me to touch someone?"

"No, that would not be beneficial. Nothing is forced upon you here.

You do whatever your heart guides you to do. You will know when it is right."

"You make things sound so easy and natural, Ashara."

"These things are natural. They are the way humanity was meant to be. The outside world has distorted them and used them for power over others. Here we do not have power over others, only ourselves and the kingdom of our own being."

"I do not understand...I only know about kingdoms and kings, wars and trade. What and where is this kingdom of my own being?"

"All of our lessons are about finding and exploring our inner kingdom. To begin we will take it a step at a time so you can follow."

Day by day Aishah let go of that which was Jezebel and began to live as Aishah, sensing it came from within her. The young students immediately loved her and she began to love them.

"We are your friends forever, Aishah. Wherever you are we are with you in spirit."

"Ashara, how can that be? What is this spirit? How can they be with me when I am not here?"

"The Great Creator over All is not physical, but spiritual. The Creator put Its Spirit in everyone. We are all spiritual children of the Great Creator. Astarte is the embodiment of the Creator's love and Baal is the embodiment of human life and harvest.

"They are consorts. Not like physical husbands and wives, but like the feminine and masculine aspects of the Creator of All. So we are all together in Spirit. Wherever we are we can never be truly separated. Always we remember we are an expression of the greatest love of all."

"How do I know this is true? Why have I not known about this kingdom within me? It all seems like a myth!"

"Yes, it does. The invisible always seems like a myth because people will believe only what they can discern with their five senses. They must touch it, see it, hear it smell it, and feel it before they decide it is real. But things we can discern with the senses can be taken away. They can be stolen, lost, or simply crumble away from age or storms. Nothing in the physical world is permanent or eternal. Only the Spirit of the Creator within us is eternal and cannot be taken or dissolved away."

"Suppose I believe it is real. How do I find it within me?"

"Aishah, what part of you knows you have a mind? What observes your thoughts?"

"Well, I guess I just know...somehow."

"Yes, the part that just knows is your Spirit. It is all knowing and eternal. It never dies. It is your true nature and it will never change.

"Come sit with me in the chapel. The harpist will play softly. We will sit quietly with our eyes closed and try to move past the thoughts running through the mind. Open yourself to knowing. It will speak to you, not in words but in soul impressions. Be patient and do not try to force it."

Aishah remembered her father saying she must do well. She was suddenly filled with doubts and thoughts of failure, of failing her father. They walked in and sat down together. The harpist began to play and they sat quietly, taking a few deep breaths. Aishah attempted to let go of her usual sense of control. After half an hour Ashara reached over and took Aishah's hand. Aishah opened her eyes and smiled.

"What did you find Aishah?"

"It seemed to take a long time for me to stop trying, stop looking for something. When you touched my hand, I did not know where I was but the trying was gone. I feel peaceful."

"Good! Wonderful! You have done well. Let us go to a cool room for a light meal, a bath in the pool, and some rest."

The words "*you have done well*" resonated throughout Aishah's whole being with relief. She would not disappoint her father.

"Some food and a bath sounds so good right now."

They walked hand in hand to the room where a light meal awaited them. They sat down on soft cushions to eat and talk.

"Aishah, you are a good student. You ask the right questions. You seem to grasp the answer even when it is an unfamiliar answer."

"Ashara, you are a good teacher. How do you explain things so clearly? Nothing I ask or say seems to fluster you."

"Learning to embody and live the spiritual teaching creates clarity. I have been teaching in this school for a few years now. I came here when I was twelve. I have loved every minute since I came here."

"How long do you think it will take me to be where you are?"

"It depends upon how much you love it! You must be willing to give up all else and embody it, make it your own."

They finished their food and went to the pool for a refreshing bath. Aishah was grateful for the time in the water, the flowers floating on the surface, and the lovely fragrances as they floated past her.

She did not talk but just let what Ashara said settle into her mind. She slipped under the surface and let the cool water wash over her head and refresh every part of her body.

Chapter 9

The days were long at the School of Astarte, filled with lessons and teachings. Even though it was rigorous Aishah found everything fascinating. She had never known about the cosmos or energy waves, or even these things that pertained to her personally. But she was finding everything she was being taught was within her. She could feel the power of it that was so different from the power of kings.

She and Ashara spent many hours together in meditation and instruction about how to use these energies. The world of Jezebel seemed far away.

"Ashara, was my world as Jezebel real? It now seems like a story someone told me about someone else. I do not know who she was."

"There is one reality, the world of our spiritual nature. It is the world of the Great Creator of All, God of All, even over Astarte and Baal. It contains all power and love from which we are to live our lives here in the physical world.

"Your life as the princess was created by the human mind. It is the physical mind where we store our memories, opinions, plans, and our perceptions of everything we see. It looks like the real world because things are solid and touchable. It feels real because we can be pleasured by it, or hurt, and even killed.

"Our thoughts and emotions are all part of that world, too. Everything is until we understand we are spiritual beings living a physical lifetime. It is like two different worlds. One has eternal reality and one does not. We can physically die, but we cannot spiritually die."

"But how do I live with both of them? How do I know who I truly am, or which one?"

"It is not as difficult as it seems. You are always Aishah, the high spiritual being, looking down upon your physical life. From that high place you bring divine wisdom. It sees to the heart of things and guides you in what to do.

"You bring divine love that takes away all fear and brings happiness and peace. It is a love of life itself. Do not let your thinking drop down into those lower levels of fear. They will cause you to forget who you are."

"Can you train me to never forget who I am?"

"Yes, immediately! Come with me and we will begin."

They went out into the garden among the flowers with their wonderful fragrances and sat down on a bench.

"Now, tell me briefly about an event in your life as the princess. What happened? And I will help you to see it from your higher nature."

They spent one of many afternoons practicing on the events of Jezebel's life as the princess. Aishah felt more trusting about her true nature. Slipping easily into her true identity as Aishah, priestess of Astarte, she could no longer imagine herself any other way. Jezebel's experiences were limited to the lower thoughts, but Aishah was filled with infinite possibility.

The year had flown by. She learned all her father had said she must. She could remember his words.

"Because, my dear daughter, the training is about spiritual power, obedience, love and humility. Those are the necessary virtues you must have to please Astarte and to be her priestess. They are not learned in a week or two."

He was right these things could not be learned in a week or two. The things that sounded strange to me have become natural and easy, even desirable. There is no other way I can imagine myself being except for the last part, Phoenician royal princess. How can I go back to being Princess Jezebel?

"Ashara, I cannot remember how to be a princess! I cannot imagine living in the palace again and not here! I remember being so resistant to coming here and now I have those same feelings about going back."

"You can always come back to visit or to stay for a while anytime you want to. Once you are a priestess of Astarte, you are always a priestess and this is your spiritual home."

A message arrived from King Ethbaal saying Jezebel would be joining a caravan going to Babylon in Mesopotamia with her brother, Eser. It would be stopping close to Byblos in two days. A carriage would be waiting for her with her guards.

Jezebel was shocked. *Babylon?* She had barely wrapped her mind around going back to Sidon and her life in the palace.

"Ashara, you must help me. Tell me how to maintain Aishah through all of the unknowns I face!"

"Come, we will practice. We will envision the caravan and all that might happen, and then Babylon. Someone here might have relatives who have been there. How much time do we have?"

"Just two days and I suppose that could change depending upon the caravan leader. Or maybe they would just forget me and go on their way without me."

They worked extensively on changing her vibration so she would be invisible to people who live at a lower vibrational level. They worked on increasing the light and Aishah's confidence to use these energies wherever she might be.

"You must trust your True nature, Aishah. All I have taught you cannot go away or fail you, but you might fail to use it. So we want to be sure that does not happen. It might mean your survival even though you have guards."

A message came that the caravan would be there in four days instead of two. They were glad for some of the pressure to be relieved.

"Good! We will polish up your self-defense practices, too."

Aishah and Ashara spent every minute they could preparing Aishah for the coming caravan and Babylonian experiences. Helpful information came from another priestess whose father had been to Babylon. Aishah was becoming excited about it all.

"In some ways I am glad for myself as Jezebel as well as Aishah. I can feel they are coming together and I am at last one person. I am more balanced and confident knowing I have are two levels of consciousness. I am not two people living in the same body. I think this would not have happened if I were going back to the palace and my old life."

On the evening of the third day, the priestesses organized a farewell for Aishah and decorated the chapel with flowers and ribbons. There was music, dancing, and a wonderful banquet. There were also tears all around as they bid her farewell.

Everyone had fallen in love with Aishah much to her surprise. Jezebel would never have thought it possible or even desired it. She might even have spurned it. Aishah's heart was wide open enjoying the love and friendships.

Hannibal and Barek came to the school gate to tell Jezebel the caravan arrived. They brought the carriage to take her. They could not believe the beautiful gentle smiling woman who greeted them. Barek could not contain his amazement.

"My lady, Jezebel! Is this you? I mean, you are so different somehow."

Quickly he stepped back and checked himself, expecting her past responses.

"Yes, Barek, it is me and I thank Astarte for the change. Please, are we ready to go?"

Hannibal smiled and bowed deeply.

"This way, Princess. The journey to the caravan is not long. Our place in the caravan is secured. There will be sufficient caravan guards as well as ourselves."

They took Jezebel's baggage to the carriage and came back to escort her there. Ashara and Aishah embraced reach other and talked for several minutes.

"I will be back, Ashara."

"Be safe my love and forever friend, Aishah."

Chapter 10

Eser was waiting in the carriage eager to see Jezebel again and for their caravan journey to Babylon. He jumped from the carriage and ran to embrace her as she and her guards approached.

"Jezebel! Is that you? You look so different. You are beautiful!"

She laughed and embraced him warmly. Hannibal held out his hand to assist her into the carriage. Eser climbed in behind her.

"I am different, Eser, and I hope I stay that way. How was your priesthood training? Tell me all about it."

"Oh, am I not more beautiful, too?"

"Um, perhaps…"

She pretended to look him over carefully. They laughed as the carriage lurched forward in the direction of the parked caravan. The guards sat on the seats behind the carriage compartment.

A space was reserved in the midst of the caravan. The surrounding distance from others befitted royalty. The driver moved the carriage into the space and the guards jumped down to take hold of the horses' bridles to quiet their prancing.

The animals in the caravan were calling to each other with huge bellowing noises. The pullers shouted at the camels and each other. The caravan began to inch forward. The camels were pulled harder to pick up the pace. Wagon wheels squawked, bumped, and rolled forward over the rough ground.

"I wonder how far it is to Babylon. I am eager to see it."

Eser had a crude map in his hand and studied it for a moment.

"It is about 650 miles, quite a long way. It will take at least three or four months to get there. I can only guess. We can ask the caravan master when we see him."

"Three or four months? I thought it would be a day or two!"

"It will be a very long journey. Caravans are slow."

Eser was always planning ahead. Jezebel no longer felt the need to complete with him. She could just appreciate him now for the wonderful help he had always been and would always be. She felt honored to depend upon him for advice and information.

"This means we will have a long time to talk about our training and our future. It has been a year since we have spoken. What a lot of catching up we have to do! I can see we have both grown up, but in different ways it seems."

"Yes, it is wonderful to be together again! We will have a lot of time. Also, Father has given me a list of things we are to observe and accomplish on this trip."

"I might have known this would not be just a pleasure trip! What do we have to do, Eser?"

"It is our usual. We check our trading goods coming and going, and watch how business is carried on throughout Mesopotamia. What other goods might we buy from India? What do they sell that might compete with ours? And you can go shopping!"

She playfully kicked him in the leg.

"Be careful, I am trained in self-defense! I can hit and kick."

"Did you learn that at the School of Astarte?"

"Yes! It is one of the less lethal things. Come on. We should get out of this carriage and walk with our guards for a while. We cannot just sit for six hundred and fifty miles."

Jezebel was out of the door and the guards immediately hopped down from their perches.

"What is it, Princess?"

"We are tired of riding and probably you are, too. Let us walk for a while."

"There might be an attack, Princess!"

"And I will make them oh so sorry! We will walk."

Eser looked at the perplexed guards, shrugged his shoulders, and offered Jezebel his arm.

The walking was stony and dusty. The caravan wagons, animals, and servants kicked up a lot of dust. The wind blew sand into their faces. The landscape was bleak high desert and there was nothing interesting to attract their attention.

Soon they climbed back into the carriage and the relieved guards back up to their perches to watch for any dangers. A crier came by announcing they would be stopping for the night. Guards would encircle the caravan to keep watch.

"We have to sleep in the carriage?"

"The seats fold down flat and extra quilts are in the storage. Just keep your head down if there is an attack."

"Do you want me to kick you again?'

"Save it. We may need it. I can kick, too. Something I learned from the Orient."

"We shall have to spar sometime!"

They both broke up in laughter.

The caravan stopped in a somewhat protected area. The guards arranged guard stations and planned watch shifts throughout the night. The caravan master came through and surveyed the individual positions. He asked King Ethbaal's driver to pull the carriage more toward the middle. Jezebel wanted to say it was unnecessary, but he strode away before she could object.

"I guess he was not taking to me!"

"You forget, Jezebel, we are royalty. Commoners do not speak to us."

She climbed into the carriage reclined on the flattened seats and quilts, closed her eyes, and began to meditate on her spiritual nature.

"Aishah, I am Aishah, and I must remember who I truly am. Astarte help me to remember and not give in to my physical nature. I remember love, gentleness, kindness, and my sister priestesses. I long for Ashara's wise counsel

and reassuring warm touch. I am all those things and I will remember every moment of the day who I am."

"Jezebel, are you all right? You seem to be mumbling about something. Are you well?"

"Yes, Eser, I am well. I am reciting my lessons so I do not forget them. Tell me about your priesthood training, all of it you can."

"Right now? The evening is upon us and the guards will bring our dinner soon."

"Yes, it is important. Right now. Did they give you a different name? Do you know the name of your spiritual nature? Tell me, please."

"My spiritual name is Ahiram, like our grandfather. I carry his spirit because he created mine. I do not know how that works, but I just accept what is told to me. I was taught we are spiritual beings from the Spiritual Creator over all gods and goddesses."

"Did the name change you? How you see yourself?"

"Since the spirit of Ahiram is within me, then his wisdom and strength are also within me."

"But are you different now because you know that?"

Before he could answer the guards came with their dinner and placed it on a small bench. They lifted the bench into the carriage and put it between Eser and Jezebel.

Eser reached for the food immediately.

"I am so hungry!"

Jezebel did not want to lose the thread of their conversation. She nibbled on some bread and figs and continued.

"What about love, Eser? Did your training include love?"

"Love is a great cosmic power that holds the universe together and everything in it. Hate creates barriers and love creates openings."

"What about personally, Eser? Does it change you personally? Inside?"

"I am not sure what you mean. I am still Eser and my interests are still the same. Explain more of this, Jezebel."

Chapter 11

"Aishah, my name is Aishah. It was given to me at the School of Astarte. It is the name I was called throughout the whole year, never Jezebel and never treated as royalty the way we usually are. Everyone there is equal. No one is treated as higher or lower, no servants or rulers. No princess, just Aishah."

"I do not understand. How could you not be Princess Jezebel?"

"Princess Jezebel was rude, haughty, spoiled, and hateful to servants. Aishah could never be that way. Aishah is love, gentleness, and a true caring for others. I practiced being Aishah for a year and found much happiness and peace."

"You do not seem different to me. You are still my sister who kicks me and threatens attackers."

"Yes, well Jezebel and Aishah merge as one. I have a softer side and a princess side. When they come together they express in a softer more centered way in whatever life brings me. This trip will be quite a test. Hopefully, Jezebel will still be there but tempered with love and spiritual strength."

"Do you have a plan as to how this will come about?"

"No, no plan. Just trusting my true nature to guide me."

They could see Damascus in the distance as they passed by going toward Ebla and Alep. Eser was studying his map and marking in more details on it.

"Why do we not stop in Damascus?"

"Because the caravan comes from Damascus. We did not get to go there because they went there first. That is why it was four days getting to us. I do not know why it happened. Our next stop I think will be Ebla. If the caravan master comes back I will ask him."

"Do you know what is in Ebla?"

"Only that the queen shared the running of affairs with the king. It has been a powerful center of civilization and a bridge between Egypt and Mesopotamia, so we may see Egyptians there, even Prince Seti!"

"Thanks so much! I can see you are going to make this trip pure joy! I do not wish to see Seti now or ever."

"Your face is red. You are blushing!"

"Stop it. I am not! But I am getting angry with you. You would make anyone's face turn red with your teasing. Prince Seti is a royal Egyptian nobody, casting about for relevance for his life."

"Well he is handsome…"

"Eser, grow up! This is not a joking matter. Please stop it now."

This was the first time Eser got such a stinging rebuke from Jezebel. He put his head down and turned away. She reached over and put her arm around his shoulder and tried not to let him know she saw tears in his eyes.

"Eser, you are one of the smartest people I know. I am proud you are my brother. Sometimes I forget you are two years younger than I am.

"Even though that does not sound like much…not like you are a child which you are not. We have grown separately this last year. We have to get to know each other again. Please, forgive me."

"I have seen how people can be friends. Our guards act like friends and joke with each other. I guess I was attempting to be like them. But maybe that is not the right way to go about it."

"Eser, I am your friend in deeper ways than the guards could never be. I love you and will always be there for you. Wherever we are we cannot be separated, even if we are in different countries. We have a bond closer than just friends or even family."

They sat quietly together until night fell. Then they wrapped themselves in the quilts and went to sleep. A few jolts of the carriage woke them as the carriage and caravan began to move. They sat up and looked out the window just as their guards brought them food to break their fast.

"Our apologies, but they ordered us not to awaken royalty. You may have to give them your own orders and free us to take care of you as you desire."

"We will eat and then you can take us to the caravan master. We will all work this out together."

"Together, Princess?"

"Yes, Hannibal. Then it will be known you are our guards, commissioned by King Ethbaal. Not just some guards to be ordered about by others."

Hannibal bowed deeply and went to the back of the carriage to wait until Jezebel and Eser had finished their food. Then their driver moved the carriage forward passing the caravan until they arrived at the front. The caravan master came to meet them as Jezebel and Eser stepped down from the carriage. The caravan master bowed politely.

"How may I serve you?"

"We were not awakened with the rest of the caravan because our guards were instructed not to awaken royalty. Our guards are commissioned by King Ethbaal and are under our instruction.

"Even though we are royalty, we wish to be treated as fellow travelers and part of the caravan. Our guards will see to our comfort and provide anything we might need. Will that be satisfactory?"

Eser was astonished at Jezebel's deference toward the Caravan master. This was not her former imperious manor. The master smiled at her and bowed politely.

"As you wish, Princess. If I can be of further service please let me know."

"My dear sister, you have changed! I have never seen you like this!"

"I am far more a princess in the caravan master's mind than if I had been haughty and looked down upon him. He will take good care of us from now on, you will see."

"Is this what you learned in the School of Astarte?"

"Yes. And many other things. They taught me where my real power resides. It is not in royalty or rank, but in love. Love is not weakness, but strength. We can teach people to fear us and weaken our position, or we can treat them with love and kindness and appear strong. It must not be an act, but a real understanding of who we are as children of the Most High Heaven.

"I did not treat you with love in what I said last evening and I regret that. It made me feel bad, too. This is the difference it makes. I would rather feel good about myself and how I treat others."

Eser smiled and hugged her.

"Our father has been strong and yet there is a kindness about him. Perhaps that is why he sent us to be trained in the priesthood, so we could learn to be like him. I always wanted to be like him, but I did not know how."

After a few weeks Ebla was on the horizon. They could see the palace on a hill and the Temple of Ishtar shining in the bright sun. The caravan stopped, but the merchants and guards continued on their own into the city.

Jezebel and Eser were enchanted looking out of the carriage windows. Hannibal and Barek had the driver move the carriage into an area where they would be safe from the shouting pushing crowds, but close enough to enjoy the experience.

Trusted merchants were selected and brought from the market to display their goods for Jezebel and Eser. Jezebel reveled in the beautiful shawls and scarves, bowls and other wares. Ever watchful, Eser kept track of the prices, as he always did. Jezebel chose a beautiful hand mirror edged in gold and Eser negotiated the price. Hannibal and Barek stood close by to be sure all was kept orderly.

"Once again we are treated as royalty and not like everyone else. I am not sure what to think about it or how to fix it."

"Jezebel, there are times when we do not know the dangers. Our guards do. Our father would have their heads if they did not see to our safety."

"There is always a division, Jezebel and Aishah, royalty and commoner. I guess it is harder than I thought to cross over those lines. At the school there were no such divisions. It was truly like the Highest Heaven of Astarte."

Chapter 12

ezebel asked the guards to take them to the Temple of Ishtar. Her heart skipped a beat as she anticipated seeing priestesses and being reminded of Ashara.

It was a long climb up to the temple and the day was hot. Immediately they were met at the gate by priests and welcomed into the cool interior.

"Please come in and we will show you our beautiful temple."

A High Priest and Priestess escorted them through the ornate sanctuary and chapels. They explained the symbols most of which Jezebel knew.

A meal was prepared and served in a plush dining room. They continued the conversation with the High Priest and Priestess about Jezebel's experience at the School of Astarte. Eser was enchanted by the whole atmosphere. He did not have an opportunity to see the interior of the School of Astarte.

Jezebel was eager to hear about Isis and the High Priestess was happy to accommodate her.

"Isis was a magical healer. She cured the sick and brought the deceased to life, and as mother she was a role model for all women. Isis was connected with the Egyptian gods and was the Syrian goddess Astarte."

She could feel Aishah living within her again as she had before she left the school. Everything about this temple reminded her of all Ashara had taught her.

"Are young priestesses trained here?"

"Yes, certainly they are. Let us introduce you!"

Some of them came forth from their dormitories at the behest of the

High Priestess. They were shy until Jezebel as Aishah opened her arms to them and they rushed to her.

Eser was a little more reserved, but he smiled at them. They greeted him with hugs and blessings, too.

"This is one of many days I shall never forget, Jezebel… or Aishah! I am still confused about that."

It was indeed a day they would not forget because this was where their carriage ride ended. They were escorted to two kneeling camels and a camel puller waiting for them to mount. The animals groaned and complained as they were lifted into the saddles.

Hannibal instructed them to lean far forward as the camel rose on its front feet, and to lean far back as the rear legs lifted it to standing. Hannibal and Barek mounted their camels. The puller tied them together with long ropes through their nose rings and connected them to the saddle of the next camel.

The caravan master stopped for a moment to inspect the loading progress.

"Why are the camels making that noise? Are they ill?"

"No, my Lady, they always do that. When they stop groaning we know their load is heavy enough and we put no more on them."

Jezebel could not help laughing in delight as she settled into the cushions of the saddle. There was a canopy over her with bright colored fringe. Everything swayed with the camel's movements.

The pullers shouted "Hut! Hut!" at the camels and the caravan slowly crawled forward toward the next city. Eser took out his map and studied it. He marked Alep on his map which was about thirty-four miles.

They had to call out to hear each other now. The atmosphere of privacy and closeness in the carriage was gone.

"Is it far?"

"No. We should be there in a few days."

"Does everything in this caravan belong to our father?"

"No, not at all. The merchants pay to be part of it out of their profits along the way and father ensures a return by paying a supercargo leader. He will take care of the receiving and disposal of the trading goods upon arrival at the cities. I understand there are paying passengers. They are the ones who ride on the bundles and then sometimes walk."

Whenever they were hungry there were figs, bread, and water in a pouch on their saddles. They would stop before evening at a caravansary just south of Alep for the night. Only farther south where the heat is intense, would they travel at night and stop at midday.

Three men came down out of the hills on horseback galloping toward the caravan. Travelers hopped down off the camel loads. The guards and other men from the caravan stood together with clubs and knives ready to fend off an attack.

The riders barged past the caravan men, slashed the ropes attaching Jezebel's camel to the others and led it away at a gallop with her still on board.

"They have taken Princess Jezebel!"

Her guards cut the ropes and got back on their camels. They shouted "hut, hut, hut," and galloped after them. Eser's camel was still tied and he could not follow them.

The caravan master hurried to Eser.

"I regret we must move on. We cannot keep the caravan stopped here."

"Sir, the brigands will be most heartily sorry. She is more than capable of defending herself. Her guards are in pursuit now. They will catch and kill them."

The caravan master looked at Eser in surprise.

"I do not understand, Prince Eser. Do you wish us to cut your camel loose so you can follow your guards in pursuit?"

"Thank you, no. They are far ahead now. If any woman can take care of herself, it is Princess Jezebel. I am guessing they expect a ransom from King Ethbaal. They will pay with their lives, not hers."

"But there are at least three of them! They have knives and they are terrible brutes. They might kill her!"

"If they do they will not get the ransom they are after. What else could be their purpose?"

"They would sell her in a slave market. A princess would bring a big price."

"Where is the nearest slave market?"

"It is in the coastal city, Ugarit, where the ships come in from all foreign ports. It is about thirty miles west from here."

Eser contemplated how to get a message to Sidon. Perhaps he could hire a horse and guard and go to Ugarit himself. His camel was still connected with the camel line. He would go with the caravan to the caravansary.

Eser told the caravan master his idea and the master immediately took him to a stable where he might at least get a horse, if not a guard. The stable owner's son, Sikhar, offered to go with him.

"Prince Eser, I am honored to escort you to Ugarit. The way is not difficult and we might be able to find your princess before anything worse happens to her. My father and I have two swift Arabian stallions for our travel. They are strong and well bred."

"My father, King Ethbaal, will be happy to reward you handsomely, Sikhar. Thank you."

Chapter 13

Eser and Sikhar rode as fast as they could first across fairly flat terrain, past Ebla, then through a low mountain pass and down to a caravan road. The horses were strong, fast, and negotiated the terrain well.

Ugarit was large with impressive palaces and temples. The waterfront was bustling and the city was a tangle of streets and alleys.

"We must find the slave sale block. Who would know?"

"A ship's captain, Prince Eser."

They located a Phoenician ship docked half way down the wharf. The captain came down from the ship when they hailed him.

"Prince Eser! I recognize you! What has happened? How may I serve you?"

"Renegades have kidnapped Princess Jezebel, taken her from the caravan near Ebla and Alep. They may be coming here to sell her in the slave market or demand a ransom from the king. We do not know for sure. Her guards went after them. I hope they caught them and rescued her by now."

"I would say those renegades are in big trouble of they captured the Jezebel I knew from a few years ago. She is a lioness!"

"Yes, she is. Please, we need to know where the slave market is."

"I will take you there. It is not easy to find. It is in an unsavory place in a dangerous part of the city. Buyers go there under heavy guard and still many are attacked, robbed, or killed."

Jezebel's guards had not yet caught up with her. She discerned the renegades were not very smart and she chose to be Aishah with her captors. She could be the old Jezebel if things became threatening.

"You wanted to capture Princess Jezebel? Oh dear, I am Aishah, only a distant cousin, of no value to King Ethbaal. I do not think he even knows who I am. He has never met me."

They were about to tie her hands when she started to cry. They stopped and threw her a quilt instead.

"Wrap up in this. You try to get away and we will kill you."

Jezebel took the quilt and pretended to dry her tears.

The captors started a camp fire. Confused that she was not the princess, they sat down to eat and discuss what to do with her.

"If she is not Princess Jezebel we will not get a ransom. So maybe we will just sell this one in the slave market in Ugarit. She is beautiful and not contentious. She should bring a good price."

At night fall after some strong drink and confident that Jezebel would not try to escape, the captors fell asleep. Jezebel pretended to sleep among the coverings from the camel saddle.

It was late when the moon was giving a soft glow to the landscape. Jezebel got out of the quilt and rose up slowly. She crept close to the snoring captors and gently slipped a large knife away from beside one of them. The captor grunted and sat up. She swung it with both hands and slit his throat. The other captors heard the stirring and jumped up just as her guards fell on them and slew them.

Before dawn Hannibal, Barek, and Jezebel caught the horses and mounted them. They gathered the ropes of the camels and tied them together. The camels naturally headed back to the caravan where there would be feed. A puller would catch hold of them when they came in and secure the ropes.

The three did not try to catch up with the caravan. They started west for Ugarit. In Ugarit they could get supplies, send a message to King Ethbaal, and decide what to do.

"Princess, you did well with the knife. I am glad you were not afraid!"

"You taught me well, Hannibal. I have never been afraid. Thank you for showing me how to use one to defend myself."

The night was cold as they followed the stars that would guide them to the coast and Ugarit.

"What did they want, Princess?"

"They discussed getting a ransom for me from the king. I told them I was not Princess Jezebel but Aishah, a distant cousin who was not even known to the king. Then they decided they would sell me in the slave market."

Hannibal was enraged.

"How did they know you were on this caravan? Someone in Sidon must have told them. Someone close to the king! But who?"

"Eser may have an idea about this. We can ask him if we ever catch up to the caravan. We can send a message to my father so he will know what happened and find the culprit."

Pink and yellow streaks of dawn were breaking across the sky and they could see their path more easily. They continued at a faster pace toward the west. Soon the Great Sea was glistening on the horizon. Barek leaned forward in his saddle.

"That is Ugarit! I can tell by the huge palace spires."

"Now to find my father's ships and send a message to him. If Eser left the caravan to follow me, he will be there or somewhere close by."

"If he is here he may look for you at the slave market. We will leave you with your father's ship captain and go to the slave market ourselves."

"Should I not come with you?"

"That is a den of rabble like your captors. We would spend most of our time beating away those who are trying to grab you!"

Jezebel never liked the idea of being left behind for her safety, but this time it sounded like a good idea. She could better spend her time in communication with Sidon.

They galloped down into Ugarit and to the docks. Jezebel dismounted and waved her guards on toward the slave market. She spotted a Phoenician ship and asked the harbor master to hail the captain.

"I am Princess Jezebel of Sidon and I need to get a message to King Ethbaal."

The harbor master bowed politely and pointed toward some cargo along the dock.

"The captain is running toward us now."

"Princess Jezebel, thank Astarte and Baal you are safe. Your brother was here and has gone to the slave market to look for you. I fear for his safety."

"My guards have gone to the slave market to find him. Eser is clever and can negotiate his way out of any situation, even if he has to buy every slave on the block to find me."

It was not long before Barek, Hannibal, and Eser were coming down the dock.

"Eser, thank gracious Astarte you are safe! I thought you might buy every slave on the sale block until you found me. Happily I was not there! How did you know where to look for me, my dear brother? You are amazing, as I have always known."

He laughed and hugged her.

"This is my friend, Sikhar, whose father owns a stable by the caravansary near Alep. He loaned his magnificent horses and his own services to find you.

Jezebel noted he was very handsome. She greeted Sikhar graciously with her thanks for his help. Eser smiled at Sikhar and took her arm.

"Come, let us go to an inn for food. I am starving! And we will tell you the whole story."

"Why are you taking my arm?"

"I am afraid you will fall into his."

"You are incorrigible!"

Barek and Hannibal declined to accompany them to the inn, but went to find a stable for the horses. The brigand's horses were old and a bit lame, but the Arabian stallions were valuable and must be looked after. They assured Sikhar they would guard them and see that they were brushed, fed, and safe.

"Eser, who knew we were on that caravan? Who sent those men after me? Was it someone in Sidon?"

"There were always rabble hanging round in Sidon. It could have been anyone who knew I was going to meet you and then go to the caravan. The royal carriage is hard to miss.

"Someone could have followed me and watched the caravan to wait for an opportunity. They most likely were targeting me, but when they saw you they thought you would be the easier prey. They did not know what a huge mistake that was!"

"Yes, it was. They paid with their lives."

They spent a few hours over dinner telling their stories. Sikhar was fascinated and felt right at home, even though he was with royalty. Jezebel had become Aishah. Eser never put on royal airs. The conversation was relaxed and they shared many details about their adventures.

In her bed Jezebel whispered, *"Royalty becoming commoners. A commoner at ease with royalty. It is wonderful when the line blurs and we are one."*

Chapter 14

"I will guide all of you back to the caravan after breaking our fast tomorrow. My father will be anxious for his horses and happy to see me return. Jezebel, would you care to ride one of my Arabian stallions?"

"I would love to ride one of your stallions! Perhaps we could trade the horses we took from the brigands for better ones before we leave. They are not in good health and a bit lame. They could use a long rest."

They sent a messenger to Barek and Hannibal to trade them for three good horses for their return.

"The extra horses will be our gift to you and your father, Sikhar. Most likely the caravan master has had the camel pullers round up our camels by now."

Jezebel was pleased with all the arrangements. She was especially drawn to Sikhar who had penetrating black eyes, curly black hair, broad shoulders, and a heroic stance.

"You are truly a princess, Jezebel! You are beautiful and smart."

She felt herself blushing.

"Please call me Aishah, Sikhar. It will be safer if people do not know who I am."

"Aishah then."

Eser and Jezebel spent the night in a room together as they were accustomed to doing. Sikhar went to the stable to care for his horses and help Jezebel's guards pick out the other three. The stable owner found three good horses to trade for the other ones which he could sell immediately.

In the morning Jezebel and Eser bought extra food provisions for all of them from the inn. They walked to the stable and the five rode off to find the caravan.

Jezebel felt joyously free as her stallion ran like the wind. Her long black hair billowed out behind her. She could not remember feeling so exhilarated and happy. Sikhar galloped beside her and they laughed into the wind. Soon they slowed the horses to a walk and began to chat.

"The caravan should be in Alep now and it will be easy to catch up with it."

Jezebel was not sure she wanted this experience to end so soon, but she knew her job was to be on the caravan with Eser and continue to Babylon. To reorient herself she deliberately turned her attention away from her attraction to Sikhar and focused on Eser.

"What is in Alep, Eser?"

"Actually, Alep is part of the Assyrian empire which is huge, prosperous, and they have a strong military with iron weapons. The markets will be organized and the shops sophisticated with expensive goods. You may not see much of it since we will be a distance outside of the city where the caravans stop."

Jezebel was disappointed. She did not want to miss seeing this city or any other city on their journey.

"I would like to see something of Alep. Perhaps we can spend a little time there and catch up with the caravan the next day."

Sikhar heard the conversation as he rode up beside her.

"I will take you to Alep! We can visit the city and then I will take you to the caravan. It will be no trouble."

"It will be an extra day. Will your father not be worried about you and the horses?"

"My princess, my father knows I will return and all will be well. He trusts me."

Jezebel blushed at the phrase *my princess*.

"Of course he does. How silly of me."

Jezebel and Eser agreed it sounded like a good plan. They wanted to see all the cities along the way and it would be a shame to skip an important city like Alep.

The ride was long and they were exhausted when they arrived at an inn at the edge of Alep. Jezebel introduced herself and Eser as the royalty they were. Rooms were made available even thought a small military presence occupied most of them.

Again Hannibal, Barek, and Sikhar went to the stables for the night to care for the horses and guard them.

A day in Alep was different and exciting. The streets were clean and straight, and the shops orderly. It was not like Sidon and Tyre where the streets were narrow, winding, and everything was bustling and chaotic.

Buildings were majestic and the military guarded all the entrances. They felt watched by unfriendly eyes wherever they went. It became almost threatening.

"Perhaps we should tell them who we are."

"I do not think that would help. We should save our identification as royalty outside of the inn in case we really need it."

It was a relief to get to the stable, mount their horses, and set out for the caravan. The guards found their recovered camels connected by ropes in the lines. The caravan was already preparing to move and the pullers shouted at the camels to start forward. They bid Sikhar farewell with profound thanks for all his help.

"Sikhar, this is for you. I might have been sold in the slave market without you. You are a true friend and thank your father."

Jezebel gave him a heavy gold bracelet with handsome dark red stones she bought in Alep. It looked regal on his dark skin. He knelt and kissed her hand.

"My honor to serve you, my princess."

He mounted his stallion, gathered the horses' ropes, and galloped away toward his father's stable. Jezebel knew part of her heart went with him.

They climbed into their camel saddles, the animals stood up with their usual groaning and lurching, the pullers were yelling, and they were on their way.

Eser noted they were headed for Tuttul, at the confluence of the Euphrates and Khabur Rivers.

"Tell me about the next place, my brother. What is it like?"

Eser pulled his goatskin journal from a pocket in the saddle and made a few notes on one page.

"I hear from the travelers it is small with a city wall surrounding it, a gate and a tower. The city has just one king, two high priests at the temple, and various chiefs. We will be crossing the river there. The cities are mostly on the north side of the river."

"How do you get a caravan across a river? Do camels swim?"

"No, it is quite shallow. We just walk them through it. The pullers know where to cross and the camels probably get their fill of water there."

He turned a few more pages.

"Ah, there is a well-known Temple of Dagon you might like to see."

"Yes! We must see the Temple of Dagon! Perhaps we will stop long enough for us to enter the city for a few hours."

"We will need to dismount and walk ahead into the city and be sure to return before our camels get to the water, or we will have to wade across ourselves."

Chapter 15

"You must talk to the travelers a lot, Eser. You learn so much! Which ones do you talk to?"

"I go to wherever they are sitting in small groups and sit down with them. I share some figs while we talk."

"But how do you understand them?"

"There are some who speak a Phoenician dialect. I can understand most of what they are saying. They chatter among themselves and I catch a few words here and there. Then I ask about the next place."

"Do they not think you are intruding? Interrupting their conversations?"

"Actually they are eager to tell me about everything. They are proud of their knowledge. Since I am around them often they sort of know me. So to them I am not an intruding stranger."

It was a longer distance to Tuttul. Jezebel and Eser napped on and off in their saddles, rocked by the swaying of the camel's gait. They ate food from their saddle pouches between naps. The land was becoming flatter and there was not much of interest to see.

Jezebel was trying not to be impatient to get to Tuttul. She remembered her lessons and meditations from the school and began to practice the energy levels and meditation sequences.

Soon tears would come to her eyes. She was missing Ashara and dreaming of the cool gardens at the school.

Jezebel realized it was close to evening and the caravan stopped. She leaned out of her canopy but could not see anything.

"Eser, where are we?"

"We are near Emar, not quite half way to Tuttul."

"Not even half way?"

She sank back into her canopy disgusted.

"Traveling by ship and on horseback has spoiled you, Jezebel! Camel caravan travel is slow. We will be gone for almost a year. Remember when we get to Babylon, we will have to come all the way back again!"

"Did you have to remind me? I am starting to wish this journey were over! It has hardly started."

"After the excitement of being kidnapped and rescued, what could this high desert land have to compete with that?"

All the camels kneeled down. Jezebel slipped out of the saddle and nearly fell onto the ground. Her legs and knees were stiff from sitting and gave out under her.

There were other caravans coming to the crossing as well. Some came up from the south and down from the north. The noise and babble of languages all around them was almost deafening.

The pullers were haggling for space as the caravans traveled side by side. Some of the pullers were trying to cut in ahead causing a squabble. The arguments ended only when the caravan master arrived to sort it out.

The travelers climbed off the bundles and found a spot to gather. They greeted each other and sat down around small fires to eat and talk. The wine and babble went on far into the night.

Hannibal and Barek set up tents and laid out sleeping quilts for Jezebel and Eser. They slept nearby to keep them safe and undisturbed by the wonderers who were drunk and staggering past.

Jezebel was sure she wouldn't sleep, but was suddenly awakened by the bellowing of the camels and shouts of the pullers that burst forth in a rising crescendo just before dawn.

Her guards gathered the tents and quilts, and packed them on the camels. The caravans began to move almost before they could get situated.

Jezebel and Eser were slightly dazed as they climbed back into their camel saddles. The camels lurched onto their feet and bellowed loudly.

Three caravans began to plod east toward Tuttul and the ford in the river. It was a popular crossing. It would take a day or two to cross once they all arrived there.

Their camel puller stopped for a moment to check on a camel that was going lame. While he tended to the camel Jezebel saw an opportunity to slide down and climb up with Eser.

"Eser, let me ride with you on your camel and talk to me before I go crazy from boredom!"

Eser laughed as he climbed down. He moved some of the pouches to her camel to make room for her to climb aboard with him.

"How can you sit here hour after hour and do nothing?"

"I am not doing nothing. Look at this."

He handed her the goat skins on which he was keeping a journal.

"I am writing everything down so we have a record of all we experience. One day I will be king and these will be useful. I will share them with you, of course."

Jezebel wrapped her arms around him and held him tight.

"Thank you, my dear brother. You are so unselfish and always taking care of me. Astarte knows I need it!"

They chatted for a while and then she laid her head down on his back and fell asleep.

She jerked up when the camels stopped. There was shouting and pullers were running. The camels went down to their knees and the pullers threw sacks over their heads.

"Get down and cover your heads! Get down!"

Eser and Jezebel dropped down beside his camel and pulled a quilt over their heads and bodies.

"What is it?"

"I think it is a storm of some kind. Do not stick your head out to see what is happening. Just hang on to me and stay covered up."

Presently there was a loud roar and a pelting of something hitting their quilt. It seemed to go on for a long time. Then it suddenly stopped and all was quiet.

The guards came to uncover Eser and Jezebel and help them up. Dirt, sand, and stones were everywhere. They shook out their quilts and robes and dusted their saddles off as best they could.

The pullers came running by snatching the hoods off the camels' heads and shouting for people to mount back onto them.

The camels stood up and the pullers were again shouting as they moved everything forward.

Chapter 16

A caravansary was just ahead. The three caravans crawled slowly toward it across the high desert terrain. Evening was coming on. The storm had delayed them and made them later than usual to get bedded down for the night.

The guards hurriedly set up their tents and shook out their quilts. Jezebel and Eser pulled some figs and bread from their pouches. Hannibal had some wine he had been saving. It tasted so good to all four of them.

"This is so good! Thank you! How far to Tuttul, Hannibal?"

"At least a day, maybe tomorrow, Princess."

"There was a buzz of conversation taking place all over the camps. Eser walked among them, picking up what information he could. He asked one seasoned traveler what the land was like on the other side of the Euphrates River.

"The land is flat and marshy in places farther east. The rivers flood each year, depositing fertile soil on the land. The rivers provide water for crops except when the floods do not come, and then there is a drought."

"Have the floods come?"

"Yes, the floods have come and are going away. The water is flowing back into the river beds now."

"Will we be able to cross at Tuttul?"

"Oh, yes. The floods are farther down the river. That is why we cross here far above them."

The morning light found the caravan already in motion. The wine was so good the night before that Jezebel drank more than she was accustomed to. That plus the bright sun was giving Jezebel a headache. She pulled a scarf down over her face hoping the effects would soon wear off.

"Did you drink too much wine, sister?"

"Do not tease me, Eser. I am in pain."

Hannibal came up to her camel and handed her a cup of liquid. She drank it and immediately the pain began ebbing away. She looked at him and laughed.

"What is this? It tastes terrible!"

"It is bitter herbs and they do taste awful, but they will quiet the painful effects of the wine. I am sorry my wine gave you pain. Perhaps it was too sweet. I will get something different for you in the next city."

Jezebel's knees were aching from riding so long, and getting on and off her camel. She clung to the straps easing herself onto the ground.

"I watched you get on and off your camel without it kneeling down. Does that not hurt your feet, Hannibal? It does mine."

"I know how to land when I jump, Princess. I will show you."

A long day stretched out before them and Jezebel began to write on a piece of goat skin. She used Eser's back as a table. She wrote the things she remembered about their voyages to Gaza and Rhacotis. She knew Eser had written about them, too, but her story would be a little different.

The next morning the walls and tower of Tuttul were in sight. The line of caravans stretched forever, lining up along the river bank like an invading army. Camel pullers were shouting, caravan masters were negotiating for a time of crossing, and all seemed like terrific chaos to Jezebel and Eser.

"How will they ever sort this out? It looks impossible. How do they know who belongs to which caravan?"

"Remember how confused we were trying to sort things out at the Trading Center in Tyre? Messengers shouting and running everywhere? But they know what they are doing even though it looks crazy to us. They have done it for decades, even centuries."

"I am glad I do not have to do it!"

"Come, Jezebel, let's go into Tuttul and see if there is anything of interest there."

They dismounted and walked toward the city gate of Tuttul. One of the chiefs of Tuttul met them at the gate and asked what business they had in his city. Jezebel and Eser politely introduced themselves and said they desired to worship in the Temple of Dagon.

"You are Princess Jezebel and Prince Eser? From where?"

"Our father is King Ethbaal of Sidon and Tyre, and High Priest of Astarte."

The chief at the gate called another chief who called another chief, who went to fetch the High Priest of Dagon. After a short time of waiting the High Priest arrived. He graciously welcomed them and bid them follow him to the temple. Jezebel breathed a sigh of relief. She did not want to leave without seeing it.

The building was not at all like the one in Gaza. It was one story with a low roof. The interior was plain with only a few faded paintings on the walls, and the statue of Dagon was much smaller. There was a strong musty smell of food, dung, and rotting wall hangings.

Swallowing her disappointment she knelt at the statue and presented it with a few wilted flowers from a basket by the entrance, and a blessing. Eser stood back with head bowed. He looked like he was going to be ill.

"Jezebel…"

"Come, brother, before you become sick. Fresh air will help. I cannot stand the smell either."

It was a relief to leave the hot stuffiness of the temple and get back out into the streets. A walk around the city helped their stomachs settle down. The market was sparse, only a few vendors. Their carpets displayed only a few items that looked dusty and worn. There wasn't much else to see so they went back out through the gate. They thanked the chief at the gate and began looking for which caravan was theirs.

"How will we find ours? Things look all mixed up!"

Barek came to them and escorted them to their camels.

"We are over here. Come with me."

He had erected the tent close to their camels while Hannibal secured more wine as he promised and brought fresh food.

"You may rest here for a while. Our caravan master has negotiated the second place in crossing. We will wait while the first one crosses. He might have gotten the first crossing if he told them there was royalty in his caravan, but he was hesitant to do that. Better to wait than to invite trouble again."

Jezebel laughed as she sat down under the tent.

"You can tell him we agree. I do not care to spend any more time with brigands!"

She would, however, have enjoyed another time with Sikhar and the stallions.

"What are you smiling about, Jezebel?"

"Never mind."

"Could it be Sikhar?"

"Be quiet and eat."

Half of the day had gone by when the first caravan cleared the water and the opposite embankment. The water was thick with mud and dung. The master instructed the pullers to wait for his signal. He wanted to let cleaner water flow through the crossing.

Eser and Jezebel climbed into their saddles and the camels lurched to their feet. Pullers were walking into water that was eighteen inches deep, shouting and pulling the first camel. The rest in the line were standing up and following along into the muddy churned up water.

There were crocodiles laying on the banks and slithering off into the water waiting for prey. Other camels thrashing around her were splashing and complaining.

Eser was right behind her shouting for her to hold on. Jezebel clutched the saddle as her camel stepped down into the water. The river did not look wide from a distance, but now it seemed to take forever to get across.

Chapter 17

From Tuttul they would start southeast. They could travel in the daytime now, but through the lower part of Mesopotamia, the temperature during the day would become extremely hot. The winter months were coming and it would be cooler to travel at night and camp through the midday.

Once on the other side of the river the first caravan was well on its way. Jezebel and Eser's caravan was climbing onto the embankment. It took a lot of jostling to get the camels into line and untangle their connecting ropes. The camel's legs and feet were caked with the mud. The pullers checked all of them to be sure they were not bitten or injured.

Soon the rhythm of the caravan movement was restored and Jezebel could relax and nap. Dreams of galloping on an Arabian stallion played in her mind, and Sikhar was smiling at her. She woke up when Eser called to her.

"Eser, you woke me from a wonderful dream. What do you want?"

"I want to tell you where we are going next. What were you dreaming about?"

"Riding Arabian stallions and galloping through the hills. I guess there are no hills here. At least I do not see any."

Eser smiled a knowing smile but said nothing about Sikhar. It was time better spent to find details about the next city in his notes than aggravate Jezebel with teasing.

"We are going to Assur on the Tigris River."

"Oh no, do we have to cross another river?"

"No, the city is on this side. Well, there may be a few small rivers to cross and a lot of flat land. Some of it may be marsh and swamp."

"How far is it?"

"About 120 miles. It will be a long ride. You can always write your memoirs, count camels, or go back to sleep and dream of Sikhar."

"Do not start that again! First it was Seti and now Sikhar. But I do have to say Sikhar was far more attractive. At least he was genuine. Seti was a phony, empty."

"Well, you will marry a king one day and neither of them are kings."

"I do not want to marry anyone! I want to be the ruler of a city on the Great Sea. Then you can sail into my port. We will trade and go shopping together. Everyone will say the great King Baal Eser II comes to visit me."

"You know Father will choose a political alliance marriage when we get back."

Jezebel sobered and took a deep breath.

"Yes, I am sure he will. He never talks to me about it. He knows I want the choice to determine my own life and future. I think he is afraid to tell me I do not have a choice. I just hope he will ask me, even though I know I must say yes."

"You want him to care what happens to you and at least talk to you?"

"Yes, and to help me make a plan about how I should be or become. What does he want me to accomplish, even under the rule of another king? I must have a purpose, Eser!"

"Yes, and you will, Jezebel. I know you."

"So, do you wonder that I dream about Sikhar even though there is no possibility of anything more than a dream? That dream holds a place in my heart regardless of what else happens. It will sustain me from deep inside. This is Astarte's gift to Aishah."

Eser was quiet for a long time. He could not help but feel her anguish at the prospect of having her life commanded by someone else, and a stranger no less. At least he knew what his future held.

Having spilled out her heart to Eser, Jezebel determined she would enjoy every mile of this journey, knowing she was free as long as it lasted. She shaded her eyes against the blazing sun and smiled.

I will love it all, even the flat barren land and wet marshes. This is my time and I will treasure it, learn from it and love it. I will remember Aishah every hour of the day.

Assur was a wonder to behold. It stood on a glorious high plateau over the Tigris River. It had temples and palaces to explore, huge markets, celebrations in the streets, and a large population. There was a moat outside of the walls and three huge gates.

After the plain buildings and smelly temple in Tuttul, Assur was fascinating in every aspect. Word came they would be spending a few weeks there, and Jezebel could not have been happier.

"Eser, we have time to explore the whole city! How did this happen that we are staying here?"

"Thank the camels. Camels need to be fed, rested, and ailments tended to. They are called ships of the desert because they can go great distances without water, but occasionally they need to pull into port and reload."

Barek came to their camels to help them gather their belongings. Hannibal went into the city to secure accommodations at a suitable inn and location for Jezebel and Eser.

They entered through the enormous stone Tabira Gate with its high arches. It spanned a large space where sellers set up a market place. Then they went through the gate in the city wall. From there the road led into a wealthy district where they would be close to temples and palaces.

After they settled into their rooms, Jezebel's first excursion was to the Temple of Ishtar. There she hoped to feel the return of Aishah as she had in Byblos. As they cautiously walked to the gate, the High Priestess greeted them with great warmth. They sat down for food and wine, and a long conversation about Jezebel as Aishah and her year of training.

"Would you not wish to stay there as a priestess forever?"

"Yes I would love to, but I am Princess Jezebel of Phoenicia and must acquiesce to my father's wishes. There is no other choice. But for now I can treasure my time with you. I am free to determine my experiences so long as this caravan journey lasts."

"Aishah, you have great courage and strength. My prayers to Ishtar shall always be with you that you continue to find happiness and the fulfillment of your dreams."

"Thank you for your prayer. It brings tears to my eyes."

Eser and Jezebel spent much time wandering from temple to temple. They even received permission from the priests of the Temple of Anu and Adad to climb the dizzying heights of the ziggurat.

"Do you think we can make it all the way to the top? Only the pyramids of Egypt are higher!"

"We can do it, Jezebel. We can stop to catch our breath. You might not want to look down as we climb. Keep looking up. The city will look very small below us. It can be a little scary at first."

Higher up the wind blew constantly. The steps were worn from wind and sand. Jezebel and Eser reached from step to step with their hands to steady themselves.

They finally reached the flat terrace at the top. The view of the rivers and the land beyond was breath taking. The Temple of Assur looked tiny below them on the point of land that jutted out into the confluence of the rivers.

Jezebel was enchanted as she looked down at the city, the city walls, and palaces. She held onto Eser's arm to keep from losing her balance.

"Do you think I could be queen of Assur? I could stay here forever."

"Not unless you could defeat the whole Assyrian empire. This is not little Phoenicia, made up of a string of city states along the Mediterranean."

"Who is the king of Assyria?"

"Forget it, Jezebel. He has a queen and over a hundred wives."

"Are you sure?"

"Yes, I am sure."

"Well, it was just a thought."

Trying not to trip or fall they made their way back down the worn uneven stone steps of the ziggurat. It was a little more difficult keeping their balance going down. They held hands to steady each other. Some steps were broken and they had to sit down and reach for the next one with their feet.

The city of Assur was protected by a double wall inside the moat that went from the river on the northwest around in a semicircle to join the river again on the southeast. As they had seen coming in through the gates, many shopkeepers set up their homes and shops in the wide space between the walls. They built apartments above their shops and swept the alley between them each morning.

Jezebel and Eser enjoyed wandering down between the walls and looking at the incredible array of goods spread out on carpets in the shops. They spent their days browsing, talking with residents, eating at various inn dining rooms and napping during the hot afternoons.

Chapter 18

Their favorite spot was the palace where the walls were thick making the rooms cooler than anywhere else in the city. There were tombs under the palace where kings and queens were buried. A city chief escorted them through the burial places and explained who the royal families were.

On their way to the inn for dinner Jezebel began to laugh.

"I guess if I wanted to be king or queen of Assur, I could look forward to spending eternity under the palace instead of in it."

"I will stay in Phoenicia, thank you."

"Oh Eser, where is your sense of adventure?"

"Anywhere I do not have to be buried under a palace far from home."

The caravan was again being readied to move on. Camels were hitched and loaded up by pullers and travelers. The first caravan had turned to the northwest at Tuttul, so there were only two caravans waiting to go southeast. All together there were now one hundred twenty camels instead of one hundred and seventy camels.

Life in Assur had been so peaceful that the constant bellowing of the camels while they were being loaded seemed deafening to Jezebel and Eser. Hannibal and Barek prepared their four camels and assisted with their climb onto Eser's camel.

Reaching into the saddle pouch Eser pulled out his notes. He was already writing about their experiences as the pullers were getting the caravan started. Jezebel was looking over his shoulder.

"Where are we going next, dear brother?"

"To Mari back over on the Euphrates River. There is a lot of territory to cover, plus lizards, snakes, bugs, and swamps. Of course you may not see them because we will travel at night when it is cooler. Now the terrain will be flatter."

"Fine. Lizards, snakes and bugs! Ugh! Now just tell me about Mari, please. What is there?"

Eser again thumbed through the pages of goat skin.

"Mari wanted to be a great trading center. The people dug canals so trading ships could come through to the center of the city and access the city markets right from the ships. It is a city built in circles. So when we get into the middle of Mari, we will be surrounded by canals coming in from the Euphrates River, going around the city, and back out to the Euphrates."

"Are there temples? A palace?"

"There may be the remains of them, but the focus has been on iron, trade, cultivation of crops, and control of the river traffic all the way to Ur on the coast of the Persian Gulf."

"If only we could get our ships here, too!"

"We will have to be content with ships of the desert until someone can dig a canal all the way to the Great Sea!"

"That will be something for you to work on when you are king. The Great King Baal Eser II Canal, going from the northwestern part of the Euphrates to Sidon and the Great Sea!"

"Well, if they can dig canals several thousand years ago, we can I am sure. Maybe we can find information on how they did it. There might be clay tablets stored somewhere."

They became accustomed to sleeping during the day in their tent and being awake at night on the camels as they traveled. The moonlight made the land bright as day much of the time, so they were not missing the scenery. They stopped at caravansaries that were active throughout the night as well as day.

Jezebel spent time reading Eser's notes and making suggestions, or filling what he might not have seen. It became a collaborative effort which they both enjoyed. They wrote during the days in the tent and napped in the camel saddles when they traveled at night.

According to King Ethbaal's wishes, they were learning how other governments, city states, and even the Assyrian empire were governed. Their bundles were stuffed with goatskin sheets filled with their journaling.

They talked about seeing Mari with its canals and markets. Jezebel was eager to see the ships come in, wondering if they were anything like the Phoenician ships on the Great Sea.

The night was ebbing and dawn revealed the huge walls of Mari. Beyond the wall the upper ruins of the famous Temple of Lions and the great royal palace could be seen.

"Why does it look so new in one area and the other side is not?"

Eser looked up his notes on Mari.

"The city has been destroyed by enemies, or flooded and washed away by the river many times over the centuries. The new part is the rebuilding taking place now. The strong smell is from the smelting and iron working places.

"I learned much of this from travelers who were in the other caravan, the one that turned northwest before Tuttul. Many of these elderly travelers have just stayed on caravan after caravan, traveling until they die."

Jezebel slid from the camel saddle behind Eser and dropped to the ground the way Hannibal had shown her.

"Perhaps their homes and villages have been destroyed and not rebuilt, so they just wander wherever they can get passage working on a caravan."

"It could well be. Towns and cities are attacked and destroyed. The people are killed or scatter and never return. Hundreds of years later a town gets partly rebuilt, like Mari, struggling to recover and continue life there."

The caravan would stay there for a week to rest the animals, water and feed them. Hannibal and Barek set up their tents just outside of the city wall. The four of them went into the city every day to explore the canals, walls, ruined palace and what was left of the Temple of Lions.

Jezebel was saddened by the sight of what had been a great trading center and wondered if it would ever recover. As they looked up and down the river there were no ships like the crowded harbors of Tyre and Rhacotis.

From the top of some of the ruined walls she could see a ship moored further southeast on one of the canals. The workers on board and in the water seemed to be dredging the canal. A resident told them it was a major canal that allowed ships to bypass the winding part of the Euphrates and come directly into the city.

The market place had been huge and was now shrunk to essential shops that sold food and grains. There were only a few that had household goods, clothing and jewelry. Much of the remaining population lived in parts of the ruins that would still offer them shelter and worked in the fields along the river.

Long ago large parts of the surviving population of Mari migrated further southeast to Sippar and Babylon, wherever they could find work and places to live.

Jezebel had learned in Byblos that Sippar was the cult site of the sun god Shamash and the home of his temple E-Babbara. She knew Inanna, Queen of Heaven, was his consort.

This made her eager to move on to find the Temple E-Babbara and learn more about Inanna in this part of Mesopotamia. The week crawled by under the blazing sun. Disappointed she settled back into writing.

"Eser, what do you know of Sippar? Is there anything said about their market or a temple?"

"I do not know. The caravan master said the river splinters into several smaller rivers there, but the main river course is on the south side of the splinters and passes Babylon. There may be remains of the Temple, but it seems Sippar was subject to the same destructive forces of the river and invaders as Mari."

As evening was coming the tent was packed onto a camel and other belongings gathered up by Hannibal and Barek. Eser and Jezebel packed their goat skin journals into the bundles with extra care and waited to mount their camels.

"How far is Sippar, Hannibal?"

"We will arrive there in four or five days. The river makes many twists and turns. The terrain is swampy in some places and rough in others. It makes traveling at night more perilous."

Chapter 19

There was little rest during the day. The flies and bugs buzzed around their heads and lizards crawled over the tent floor. Jezebel wrapped up in a quilt pulling it over her head trying to get a little sleep, but it was too hot for sleep. Eser worked on his notes, swatting at the flies and fanning the air over Jezebel in her quilt.

Traveling at night held little relief from the challenges. The winter months were waning opening the way for the rise of intense heat. The water in marshy places created by winter rain and a swelling river started to drain away making the footing muddy and slick.

The caravan made a brief stop early in the day near Sippar. Jezebel, Eser, and Barek eagerly hurried toward Sippar. While they were gone some travelers from the other caravan ahead of them had dropped back and were wandering about. Hannibal was sure they were coming to rob them so he stayed behind to guard to the camp site.

"Here, over here! These are the rich ones! I saw them go into the city."

"They have guards, you fool!"

"I do not see any guards…"

Hannibal stepped out from behind them, grabbed them both, and killed them with his knife before they could get loose. He dragged their bodies behind a pile of fallen wall stones and covered them with debris and dirt.

There was little in Sippar to see. The other half of the city which might have held the temple site was across the river. Jezebel hoped to find more about the sun god, Shamash, and see the Temple of E-Babbara but it was not to be.

It seemed there was less and less to see as they traveled southeast. The old cities were half destroyed. There were no viable temples or priests to tell her about things, only workers in the fields and a boat or two trolling the river for whatever reason.

"Do not worry, sister. Babylon will yield all we could wish for. Babylon is a thriving metropolis and we will be there for a few weeks. We may even find more about Sippar and Shamash there. Babylon took over the whole area, all the cities, industries, and shipping. The territory is called Babylonia."

Jezebel brightened up. Babylon was not so far away and she was ready for some new excitement. Climbing around on rocks and fallen down walls looking for anything, any clue, was yielding nothing but skinned knees and sore hands.

A huge caravansary awaited the caravans just outside of Babylon. The other caravan traveling ahead of them was already there. There were greetings among the camel pullers and travelers who had met far back in Tuttul at the river crossing.

All the camels were kneeling and there was a flurry of activity unloading them. Wagons and drovers were waiting to carry goods to the market places. Barek had gone into the city ahead to find a suitable inn and rooms for the four of them.

Hannibal secured a carriage to take Jezebel and Eser into the city of Babylon. The city walls were so wide their tops were used for a race track. The enormous Ishtar Gate was the most amazing of all to Jezebel. The bright blue glazed bricks decorated with depictions of bulls, lions, and golden dragons were dazzling to the eye and took her breath away. Even Rhacotis and the Egyptian pyramids had not enchanted her like this gate.

It was a long way across the city to the inn. Jezebel could not wait to soak in a bath and scrub the stink of camels off her skin and out of her hair. When she arrived in her spacious room, a servant brought fresh tunics and sandals, soaps and fragrances, and helped her wash.

When Jezebel was ready to get out of the pool, the servant wrapped her in a large towel and led her to a massage table where fragrant oils were rubbed into her skin. Fatigue caught up with her as she relaxed. She collapsed onto a soft bed in the next room. The servant covered her with a light quilt and left her to sleep.

Late in the evening Eser came to her rooms to escort her to the dining room.

"After a bath I slept all day. Did you as well?"

Jezebel laughed and nodded as she slipped into the new sandals.

"I only remember getting out of the pool and being helped onto the massage table. That is all! Somehow I made it to the bed and was asleep before I collapsed on it. I am starved!"

"Dinner is this way."

Jezebel took Eser's arm as she went with him to the large dining hall. They were escorted to a beautiful table covered with bowls of fruit and vases of flowers.

"Where do these flowers came from? I have not seen flowers like these since we left Byblos."

"They come from the hanging gardens of Babylon, my Lady. You must see those gardens for yourself. They are a marvel to behold."

"Early tomorrow, dear sister, we will start out to see the city! Hannibal and Barek will bring the carriage. Our innkeeper will give us directions and a list of sites. We may start to be princess and prince to gain easier access and even protection."

"Eser, you are a master planner! Early morning it shall be. I still need to sleep tonight, still regaining my strength. I feel like I held my breath for the entire caravan route."

"Well, we have to go back over that same route to get home. You may want to breathe more often."

"I have a plan for getting home. I will tell you about it later, maybe when we are in Ur."

"You have a plan? Why wait to tell me?"

"Well, it is not quite complete. I have more thinking to do. When I tell you, you can decide whether to accompany me or not."

"What? I always accompany you! Jezebel, we have always been open with each other! Why the mystery?"

"You are always the one who has a plan. Now it is my turn! I need a little more time and information. Please, trust me."

"Trust you? Yes, of course I trust you. I just do not understand this secretive behavior I have never seen before."

"I had plans when we were kids at the palace I did not tell you about."

"If you had told me back then, I could have kept you from always being caught by the palace guard."

"Oh, and here I thought it was you who told them!"

"I would never have told them! I did not know. But seeing how they caught you helped me learn how plan better and get past them myself."

"You sneak!"

"Well it enabled me to get information for both of us. I was able to go to the Trading Center in Tyre and return before they knew I was gone. I pretended to be searching for the horse they thought somehow got away. Actually I had borrowed it from the stables.

"And then I went to the docks in disguise and spoke to captains and sailors where I learned a lot. Did you think I just pulled all of that out of my own head?"

Jezebel and Eser laughed all through dinner and back up to the rooms as they reminisced about their childhood escapades at the palace.

The next days were full of discoveries as they traveled the streets, gates, markets, temples, and palaces of Babylon. It was safe enough for them to travel as royalty. Many doors opened for them and conversations with high officials as well. Eser was filling pages of goat skin with information he would need as king of the city states throughout Phoenicia.

Jezebel was listening and taking in the sense of what royalty and rule were about. She could feel their slight condescension because she was only a princess, but she ignored it. This would be the pervasive attitude regardless of what rank she had, even queen.

"Eser, has Father commanded we go all the way to Ur and the Persian Gulf, or might we decide to return home from Babylon and take a different route?"

"What a strange question, sister. Does this have something to do with the plans you will not tell me about?"

"All right, I will tell you if you promise not to tease or tell me it is stupid."

"I promise. Now what are you thinking?"

Chapter 20

"I want to go home, but not in a camel caravan trudging back up the Euphrates River we have just traveled down. What will we learn from that? What a waste of time."

"Yes, I understand your thinking and no, it does not sound stupid. So how do you propose we shall return home? What different way is there?"

"I propose we go home on horseback along the Tigris River. It would take us weeks instead of many months with the caravan. There are probably some small city states where we could get food supplies. Being close to the river water would not be a problem. We can buy four horses and two pack animals. I will ask our caravan master if he can help us."

"He will insist we stay with the caravan or our father will have his head on a pike. However, it is an interesting idea. I will not call it stupid, but perhaps risky."

"Yes, it is risky since we will not have a guide and only Hannibal and Barek to protect us, but we did not have any other security in the caravan. Those brigands cut my camel lose and dragged me off into the hills with no interference from the caravan guards."

"Yes, and the caravan master said he could not delay the caravan to go find you. So I stayed on until Sikhar's stable came into sight. That was fortunate."

"You and I can fight alongside Hannibal and Barek. People on fast horses might not be tempting prey like slow plodding camels. I think we can do it!"

"Do you not wish to see the ziggurat in Ur and the seaport there? The city is thriving and is larger than Babylon. It has canals like Mari and a huge market place since it is on both a seaport and caravan route."

Jezebel sighed and sat with her fist under her chin for a while.

"It might be wonderful, but I have seen my fill of markets and buildings. We already climbed one ziggurat and walked by the silted up canals at Mari. Ur is built on marsh lands with more bugs and lizards. We can tell Father I became ill from the marsh lands and damp air. We decided to return home."

They told the caravan master Jezebel was ill from the dampness and decided to return home by the quickest way.

"Well you could fly, but there are no birds here large enough to carry you. With horses perhaps you could make it in a few weeks if all goes well. But as you know everything does not always go well. However, if you insist, at least I can trade your camels for good horses and pack animals."

Eser and Jezebel discussed their plans with Hannibal and Barek that evening. They were also skeptical. They knew the king would not be happy with their plans to travel the Tigris instead of the Euphrates.

"There are few or no well-traveled caravan roads or caravansaries. We would be alone. Your father will have our heads if anything happens to you. He may do that anyway. Let us sleep on it tonight and we will talk again in the morning."

Jezebel was wakeful and tossed on her bed. Plans kept running through her mind, even whether or not she could see Sikhar again. But she knew that was not an option. There was no point to it and Eser would never let her hear the end of it!

In the morning the caravan master, Hannibal and Barek had a meeting and discussed Jezebel's plans for a return up the Tigris River. The caravan master worked out a possible route through the area and the cities where they could resupply their stores. He also knew areas to avoid that had quicksand or deep holes swirled out by the river at flood stage.

He gave them the names of his contacts there in case they needed help or directions. But he knew them many years ago. They might not still be alive.

Jezebel could not believe her good fortune that the caravan master was so knowledgeable and helpful. Hannibal and Barek were somewhat mollified by realistic plans and assurances. However the plans included going to Ur with the caravan. The caravan master noted her perplexed look.

"You will take a small ship from Ur to Lagash which is on the Tigris and continue northwest along the Tigris from there. Horses will be there for you when you dock. If you attempt to cross to the Tigris from Babylon, you will encounter miles of swamps making your journey perilous.

"From Lagash, you will avoid them. Princess, I hope you can see the sense of this and be assured I have your best interests at heart. Your father would have my head if I let you cross those swamps filled with crocodiles, snakes, and other vermin. Please, come with us to Ur.

"Yes, I understand and thank you. You have been most understanding and helpful. We will continue with you to Ur. I will look forward to being on a ship again. I have sailed the Great Sea and now the Persian Gulf. It all feels right."

Eser listened to all of this without comment, but Jezebel could tell he was relieved at the new plan. He knew about the swamps and did not relish trying to find their way through them to the Tigris River.

"Breathe easy, Eser. Reason has triumphed emotion and I see the good sense of following the caravan master's plan."

"Dear sister, this is actually the first time I have seen you capitulate and allow someone else to lead the way!"

"Oh, not true! I gave way to climbing through the ship's hold and the cargo, and helping you keep the records. I even gave up shopping for you."

"Tell me the truth, Jezebel, will you follow the caravan master's plan or do you have something else up your sleeve?"

"Yes, as far as Lagash. From there we have the river to guide us, so we may have to modify a few things as we go along. Trust me, Eser, I will do nothing we do not plan together. You are my true friend and I will not violate our trust."

The caravan stopped briefly near Uruk. Jezebel and Eser could see the remains of the mighty red stone ziggurat and what was left of walls and fragments of palaces, but again it had been in decline for centuries.

It was a relief to arrive in Ur with its thriving seaport and markets. They spent a few days touring Ur until the ship and a crew were ready. The ship was not as large as the ones on the Great Sea, but it was swift. They would sail close to the coastline until turning into a bay. It led to a water way that would take them close to Lagash.

Being on the gently rocking ship soothed Jezebel's longing for the sea. It allowed her to rest and renew her enthusiasm for the trip home. Eser stood at the bow as they moved out into the gulf waters and turned northwest into the bay. He, too, was restored and felt again his eagerness to have an adventure, to see the Tigris and all they would encounter along the way.

Hannibal and Barek remained vigilant even on the ship. Their charges were of a royal family and the seamen were strangers. They did not know how much the caravan master had told the seamen about their passengers.

Eser chatted with the seamen about their route and where they would dock. He asked each where they came from and if they had families. The seamen began to relax and be willing to share their stories. Jezebel knew Eser would add all of this to his notes. He never stopped working and learning.

In the evening the ship docked and as promised there were horses and pack animals waiting. The young man who brought them also acted as their guide into Lagash where they would spend the night. The inn there was old and the stable was barely able to contain their six animals.

Jezebel did not mind the spare accommodations. They were on the journey into the unknown and it was exhilarating.

Chapter 21

Lagash, like Uruk and many other cities they visited along the way, was long past its heyday and importance in the area. Kings took over large territories engulfing these small cities. They were absorbed into the greater empires and their structures left to disintegrate.

Jezebel and Eser collapsed onto thick mats on the floor of the inn with their bundles tucked around them for warmth and safety. Hannibal and Barek bunked with the horses and pack animals to feed them and insure they would not be stolen.

In the morning Eser brought out a list the caravan master had given him of places they could stop along the river.

"We will go to Eshnunna, crossing the Tigris half way there to avoid the marshes. From there we will cross back over the Tigris and head northwest to Assur. It is spring and the heat will be rising, but not the river, so crossings to the northwest should be shallow and plentiful."

"Any crocodiles?"

"Probably. Just don't step into the water yourself. Let your horse do it."

"I have no intention of wading…but a bath would be nice."

"You would be eaten!"

They both broke out laughing.

Barek and Hannibal bought food at the tiny market in Lagash and readied the animals to start up the river to find a crossing. A local man in the market place told them about a good place to cross opposite Kish.

They would pass a lake after the crossing that would mark the halfway point to Eshnunna.

As they saddled the horses Jezebel looked around dubiously at what must have been a larger stable and surely a more substantial building.

"How did you feel safe sleeping in here, Hannibal? The place could have fallen down on your heads while you slept!"

"Yes. Even so it is better than unprotected in the open. The horses would have warned us."

The horses were full of energy, bobbing their heads, shaking their manes, and calling to each other. Jezebel mounted her horse while Eser held its bridle, then climbed onto his while Hannibal held its bridle. The pack animals were loosely tied together. Hannibal and Barek swung onto their horses and they started off at a brisk pace.

There were tributaries of the river on either side of them as they pushed forward to find the crossing the man of Lagash described. It was fast becoming hot and humid. They needed to get to the crossing and onto dryer land.

Barek saw the crossing and went on ahead to test the depth of the water and the footing for the horses. It was shallow and Barek poked the muddy banks looking for crocodiles. Soon he motioned them forward. The horses waded gingerly in the mud and jumped onto the far shore.

A few miles more and they passed the small lake on their right. The way was becoming dry and arid as they rode northwest in anticipation of finding Eshnunna. They paralleled the northern bank of the Tigris as best they could. There were grasses and flowers here and there.

When the sun was high they stopped to rest and allow the animals to graze for an hour or two. Eser took advantage of the stop to write. Jezebel snoozed under a lean-to tent.

As they continued, the remnants of a caravan road appeared out of the weeds before them. It had been a long time since anyone except perhaps a lone rider had traveled it. Evening was coming and the low buildings of Eshnunna could be seen on the horizon.

Barek went on ahead to find an inn and market place. Almost nothing was there. He rode through the ruins until he came upon a roofless building with high walls that could have been a temple. Nearby were a few low tents that constituted a kind of market place.

Hannibal looked at the caravan master's list of names. He asked a man who was sitting under the tents eating figs if he knew one of them.

"Died...long time ago."

The four brought their animals and belongings into the place with high walls and camped there for the night for protection. Hannibal sorted out their remaining food and built a small fire.

"We have enough food to get to Assur. We should start out before dawn. The caravan road is easy to see now and there is water and feed for the horses and pack animals."

Jezebel hoped to see the Abu Square Temple and Shrine in Eshnunna but only the outlines made by the crumbled walls were visible.

"Nothing lasts forever, Eser. We are seeing the rise and fall of cities and empires. They all eventually fall into dust and ruin. It is sad for the people living in them. I wonder what happened to the populations or where they went. There must have been thousands of them just disappearing into the wind and sand."

Eser made a few notes on a scrap of goat skin by the light of the fire before they went to sleep. Before it was light they struggled to awaken, ate a few figs and started out. In a few hours they came to a place where they could cross back over the Tigris and continue northwest to Assur.

It was high desert country where there was some vegetation and water from the river. The temperature rose high during the day. In the afternoon they stopped and put up the tent. The animals nibbled on some nearby bushes and grasses. Barek washed their eyes and noses with water from the river and adjusted their packs.

Toward evening they continued until they came to some ruins and a small band of three men camped there. They drew knives as Hannibal and Eser approached them.

"What is this place?"

"It is Ekallatum and it belongs to us. Who are you?"

"I am Prince Eser of Sidon, traveling home after a long journey. Peace be unto you."

"Are you traders? Do you have trading goods with you?"

Barek became wary and rode up beside Eser

"No, we are just travelers."

"Will you sell the woman?"

Jezebel heard this and put a hand on the long knife Hannibal had given her at the beginning of the journey.

"She is Princess Jezebel, sister of Prince Eser and daughter of King Ethbaal. She is not for sale."

One of the men approached her and took hold of the bridle of her horse.

"She looks nice. We will give a good price."

Hannibal dismounted and grabbed the man's arm.

"Let go. She will kill you."

The man laughed and did not loosen his grip. Jezebel eased the knife partly out of her saddle pack. When he looked back at Hannibal she whipped it out and grazed his arm. The man fell back in shock.

Jezebel was blazing with anger.

"I do not wish to harm you further, so let go of my horse, back away, and leave us in peace!"

Hannibal remounted his horse and they rode away before the three could decide to threaten them further.

Chapter 22

I t was good to see Assur in the distance. It was almost like coming home to be in a familiar place.

As they entered the city Jezebel sought out the temple. She wanted to see the High Priestess who had welcomed her many months ago. A serving woman met her at the entrance to the temple.

"Welcome. The High Priestess is quite ill and cannot come to you."

"I am Aishah, priestess of the School of Astarte. Please, take me to her!"

The woman bowed and guided Jezebel through the rooms to where the High Priestess lay on a bed of pillows and silks. She opened her eyes as they approached her bedside.

"Aishah, is it you? I can hardly believe my eyes that I should see you again before I die!"

"Please, High Priestess, allow me to minister to your illness and begin a healing. There is no need to die."

The High Priestess reached out to take her hands.

"Are you skilled in the healing arts, Aishah?"

"Yes. Let us begin."

Jezebel continued to hold her hands. She closed her eyes and called upon Aishah, Isis, and Astarte to gather the energy and light into focus. She could feel the High Priestess' body begin to respond with its own healing power. After an hour the High Priestess was sleeping, breathing easily, and the color coming back into her face.

Jezebel returned to the temple the next morning to find the High Priestess on the front steps.

"It was really you, Aishah! I thought perhaps in my fevers I had dreamed of seeing you."

They fell into each other's arms and walked back into the temple together, arm in arm. The serving woman brought them wine and food as they sat talking. Eser came to the temple to tell Jezebel they would be leaving the next day.

"Please join us, Prince Eser, Priest of Astarte. I am sorry you must leave so soon. I did not think I would ever see Aishah again. Last evening she helped me heal my illness. I was not successful at doing it alone. She came to me just in time."

Eser smiled and sat down with them. He discerned that was a holy gathering and joined them in speaking of Higher things. He remembered to call her Aishah. Whatever Eser learned in his priestly studies, he had become a perfect counterpart. Jezebel was seeing this side of him for the first time and her pleasure shone in her words and smile.

It came time for them to part and they conferred blessings upon each other as they hugged and kissed. Hannibal and Barek were waiting for them at the city gate at dawn.

Supplies were replenished and the animals were rested and eager to go. The horses stomped and snorted as the city gates opened and they departed at a brisk trot.

Jezebel insisted they go to Nimrod which was not far. She had enough of the destroyed palaces and ancient ruins. Nimrod was the shining jewel of Assyria with beautiful buildings, market places, and palaces.

"If I am to marry a king, I want to know what the highest and best of a kingdom looks like. I want to hold an image in my mind to manifest something glorious for my future."

"Sister, you need to explain to me what holding an image is and what it does."

"Eser, our minds are powerful. Empires are built because someone has an image, a dream, of a great empire. They are focused on that image. They see it day and night and know it will come to be their experience.

"Nimrod did not just grow up on its own. Someone had and still has an image of what it will be. Then they build according to that image.

Most people do not have an image of something great so they do not build anything great."

Eser frowned and thought for a while.

"Well, would you say I have an image?"

"Yes you do! You put your images in writing. You write them down, creating a story. It is a wonderful way to hold the image as you build it in your mind. I hope you will always be building and expanding on your dream and never stop."

Nimrod was everything Jezebel hoped for. It was glorious in every way, full of art, mosaics, and colors as well as stupendous buildings and monuments. They found a beautiful inn in the middle of it all to rest and stay for a period of time.

Hannibal and Barek secured the animals in a reliable stable where they would be safe and well cared for. This freed them to join Jezebel and Eser at the inn and relax a little from their vigilance for a time.

King Ashurnasirpal II made Nimrod his capital, building a large palace and many temples. Any buildings fallen into disrepair were rebuilt and a wall five miles long surrounded the city and grand palace. His son, Prince Shalmaneser, enlarged the palace to twice its original size adding two hundred rooms and began building the Great Ziggurat with an adjacent temple.

The four toured the construction sites to watch hundreds of workmen busy constructing the walls, laying out plans, and measuring areas. Others were fitting gigantic stones into place while artists created huge designs with colored tiles, enamels, jewels, glass, metals, and bricks to decorate them. The reflection of the sun on them was stunning.

Jezebel and Eser requested an audience with Prince Shalmaneser and to their surprise the request was granted. Jezebel bought robes, tunics, sandals and jewelry for herself and Eser to wear for the occasion. They were introduced as Prince and Princess, and brought greetings from King Ethbaal of Sidon and Tyre.

Eser explained the long journey they had been on throughout

Mesopotamia and their travels on the Great Sea as far as Rhacotis. Prince Shalmaneser listened with interest and regaled them with his plans for his city and empire. He took them on a tour of the palace and showed them the beginnings of the two hundred rooms that were under construction.

Prince Shalmaneser ordered wine at one point for refreshment before their departure. Then they bowed, bidding each other farewell. Servants guided Jezebel and Eser out to the front gate of the palace where Barek and Hannibal were waiting with a carriage. Jezebel flopped down on the carriage seat.

"I am thrilled and exhausted! I did not think we would be so graciously received but we were! And what a marvelous experience it was."

"Yes, it was! Let us go back to the inn for some rest and food. I want to get my notes out and write down all we heard about building a city!"

"Do you see what I mean about holding the image, the dream? I will help you!"

They both poured over the goat skin as Eser wrote as fast as he could.

"You are talking faster than I can write, Jezebel! Can you slow down?"

"Well, I am excited and eager to go back out into the city to see what else we can find…all right, I will slow down."

They had a leisurely dinner at the inn and decided tomorrow would be a good time to continue their search. Eser started listing the sites and markets places. He thought they might even be able to find a guide.

Chapter 23

First thing in the morning a man from Prince Shalmaneser's palace arrived at the inn through a back door and approached the owner.

"I must speak with the prince and princess of Sidon and Tyre! Privately please."

The innkeeper did not recognize the man.

"I do not know who this man is. He said he is from the palace. Do you wish to speak with him or shall I send him away?"

"If he is from the palace he may be risking his life by coming here. Let us speak with him."

Jezebel and Eser cautiously agreed to meet the man in a private room to the side of the dining room. He came in from a back door, bowed low, and kept his face covered. He kept his distance so as not to be intrusive.

"Prince and Princess, I come to you in secret because I know of your meeting with Prince Shalmaneser. He is a warrior who is planning many campaigns, some of them against Phoenicia and Israel. I do not believe you are safe here. He may be planning some advantage against them that includes using you as hostages. Be aware and be careful. I must leave now."

He disappeared out of the same back door into an alley and was gone.

Jezebel and Eser were in shock at this sudden threat to their safety.

"I do not know what to think about this. He seemed sincere and did not ask any reward for himself."

"He certainly has risked his life."

The innkeeper did not recognize the man and was worried for his guests. At Eser's request he sent a message to Hannibal and Barek in their respective rooms. Jezebel told them about the visit from this man.

"Hannibal and Barek, did you see anyone around our carriage while you waited for us at the palace? A man who kept a hood up and covered his face?"

"There was a man who walked by, but did not look our way. Now that I think of it, I saw him again as we came back to the inn. Still he did not look our way but hurried on going about his business."

Eser was most concerned.

"The first thing we must do is move out of this inn to a less prestigious one."

"I will shop for us. Hannibal can take me to a market where I can buy clothing similar to what the common population wears. We will not run away like scared rabbits. Just keep a low profile."

Eser and Barek gathered their belongings into a small carriage. The inn keeper suggested a few inns in another part of the city that would be plain but adequate.

Jezebel brought back the purchases and they changed into them before they got into the carriage. The inns the innkeeper suggested were across the city. There was one that was in a good place and looked safe. Eser went in to look it over.

"It is good enough. Let us check in, bring our belongings in, and dismiss the carriage. We will continue our tour of the city on foot and leave quietly in a day or two."

Jezebel hid the upscale clothing they wore to the royal audience in a bundle in the inn wine cellar. She kept the jewelry with her. It was not a happy turn of events, but they had only an anonymous warning with no further indication of a threat.

Barek and Hannibal did some surveillance work of their own as Eser and Jezebel wandered through the city following Eser's list of sites. Nothing seemed amiss, but they continued to be watchful.

The day they decided to leave Barek and Hannibal readied the horses and pack animals and led them out through a dung gate of the city. Jezebel and Eser followed them at a distance and turned to exit by a different gate.

They breathed a sigh of relief as they passed through the gate seemingly unnoticed. Barek and Hannibal met them with the horses and they were on their way.

Their next stop would be to cross the Khabur River at Nawar and go toward Haran. Their horses were fresh from the stay in Nimrod and they traveled at a quick pace.

Jezebel was interested in the tales she heard at Tuttul about the Eye Temple at Nawar, but she knew there would be nothing left but a few stones where palaces and temple walls had been.

They turned toward Nawar to cross the Khabur River and rode into the foothills of the Taurus Mountains.

Barek and Hannibal decided it would be good to camp on the other side of the Khabur River for a few hours during the heat of the day. It was a longer trek from there to Haran and there were no caravansaries or villages on the way. Their food stores were good and would last until they got to Haran.

From there the four planned to travel south to Alep, then Ebla to Ugarit on the coast. The plan was to leave the animals with Sikhar and take a Phoenician ship from Ugarit back to Sidon.

Jezebel tried to hide her pleasure at the possibility of seeing Sikhar again but Eser was not fooled. He teased her as he had before.

"Enjoy your freedom for another month before we arrive back in Sidon and our palace duties there."

"I wish you could just leave me at Byblos to return to the School of Astarte for a time. I need to recover my mind. Ashara will help me to return."

"I am sure the Phoenician ship will stop at Byblos. You can disembark there and go to the School. I will tell Father."

"What will you do, my brother? Will you go to Sidon and wait for me there?"

"I will be in Sidon unless Father has other plans for me. How long do you want me to wait?"

"Send me a message if that happens."

"I am concerned you may not return at all."

"It is a tempting thought…"

It was a long dusty way to Haran through foothills and valleys, but the terrain was far more interesting than lower Mesopotamia. Hannibal told Jezebel and Eser about the ancients Abram, Sarai, and his father Terah.

"They came the way you chose, Jezebel. They followed the Tigris River from Ur all the way to Haran. His father, Terah, was from Haran and wished to return there to spend his last days. When his father died, Abram, Sarai, and Abram's nephew Lot traveled south through Canaan, now Israel, to Egypt."

Eser was puzzled.

"I have heard this story before. Abram's god called him to do this but I do not know why they went on into Egypt."

"Because there was a terrible famine in Israel. In Egypt there was plenty of food and water. They returned to Canaan many years later. Over a thousand years of history has happened since then which resulted in the creation of Israel."

"Wonderful! I chose their way! So I was not wrong or crazy."

Jezebel listened to the conversation with interest convinced she would never want to go to Israel.

"It seems Israel is forever at war with someone. Could they not just settle down and build their own country?"

"Israel has ten tribes formulated in the time of Joshua. There are actually twelve tribes, two of them are in Judah and the other ten in Israel. Judah has peace between their two tribes, but Israel's ten tribes are always arguing and fighting for power. That makes Israel vulnerable and Judah rock solid."

"I suppose it seems strange to others. We have traveled throughout Mesopotamia and down the coast of the Great Sea to Rhacotis and back. It all has no obvious purpose except for our education. We are not looking to make war or take over someone else's territory for power."

Eser smiled because he knew if someone wanted to take over Phoenicia there would be battles. His father had already murdered the king of Tyre for those same reasons, to grab his territory for prosperity and power. He would know how to defend Phoenicia.

At the end of the day Haran was on the horizon. They came to a great crossroads, intersections of main roads coming in from all directions and leading out again.

Barek trotted his horse ahead to see which road would take them into Haran.

Hannibal stayed back with Jezebel and Eser.

"Haran is a great trade center as you can see by the main roads intersecting here. Caravans come from all directions bringing goods to Haran to be carried to the northern passages. Those strange cone shapes you see in the distance are the beehive houses, residences where the locals live."

Jezebel shaded her eyes to see them and looked quizzically at Hannibal.

"Why those shapes? I have never seen anything like them before."

"There are miles of rocks shaped in that cone style, some contain whole cities. Cappadocia is one of those cities. They may be mimicking the style of the rocks or they may have discovered some advantage against the heat, rain, and wind. They carve their homes right into the rocks. The homes have lasted for centuries."

Chapter 24

"Hannibal, how do you know so much about these places?"
"Ah, I traveled extensively with your father when I was a boy and he was a younger man. He wanted to know all he could about neighboring countries and their cities. This is why he sent the two of you on the same kind of journey. Has he never mentioned this to you?"

"He has not."

Jezebel did not know whether to be interested, perplexed, or jealous and angry that she and Eser were not told.

"Eser did you know? If you did and never told me I will kill you on the spot!"

"No, dear sister, I did not know. Father never mentioned why we were going on this journey except to learn. I told you when we started out on the camel caravan. If he had shared his story I would have."

"So you did. I will not kill you."

"Jezebel, I tell you everything I know, always. I have not and will not keep anything from you."

They entered the city near a huge palace that dominated the central area. The markets were tucked in all around it. As they wandered through the market stalls, Jezebel kept looking for temples, a temple of Isis, Astarte, or Baal. There were none.

"Hannibal, why are there no temples to gods or goddesses here?"

"Haran is over four thousand years old and grew out of the caravan crossroads. There is little in the way of local social life or worship. Most of the local people run the markets. There is only business here, nothing else."

"How strange! Most cities worship a god or goddess who would watch over them and insure their harvests and prosperity. So there is nothing like that here?"

"This is what happens when there is no society, only trade. I do not know of any other city like this."

They gathered supplies at the market. Jezebel brought out the bundle of clothes she bought when they visited Prince Shalmaneser in Nimrod. She found a clothing kiosk in the Haran market and sold them to the merchant who was happy to receive such beautiful items. Eser watched over the transaction. They brought a good price.

The next morning they left for Alep, Elba, and Ugarit. Seeing places they had already visited many long months ago felt like going home.

They stopped in Alep and sent a message to Sikhar to meet them in Ugarit and take the horses and pack animals as their gift to him and his father.

Ugarit and the Great Sea were a welcome sight. The sea air was refreshing and the familiar noise of the docks called to them.

Sikhar arrived and found them near the docks where he knew they would be. Jezebel jumped off her horse and flew into his arms.

Eser smiled his *"I told you so"* smile at Hannibal and Barek.

Their reunion was exciting and they regaled Sikhar with the stories of their journey.

"I am surprised you are still alive going through the Mesopotamian territory. Not eaten by crocks or bugs! But I do know Jezebel can take care of herself and all of us too!"

Their banter over food and wine was pleasant. Jezebel enjoyed spending time in Sikhar's company. His energy and attention were exhilarating.

They stayed in Ugarit for another day until a Phoenician ship was ready to sail. The morning the ship was ready to sail, Jezebel knew walking away from Sikhar was the hardest thing she ever had to do up until now.

He watched as they boarded the ship, waved, and then turned to get the animals. He rode Jezebel's horse and led the rest. It somehow soothed his longing. He was certain this time he would never see her again.

The next port of call was Byblos, a short sail away. Jezebel was eager to see Ashara and reluctant to leave Eser. She was afraid they could never again be as close as this journey had brought them. Life would intervene and the future was so uncertain. First she had to leave Sikhar and now Eser. She needed to find her inner Aishah again.

Hannibal sent a message to the school and they were all at the gate to greet her. Tears streamed down her face when she saw Ashara. They ran into each other's arms and kissed each other's cheeks.

"Come! A bath and our room is ready."

"A bath! Yes! I must smell like a horse or a ship, I am not sure which."

What a luxury to plunge into a warm sweet smelling bath with flowers floating all around and soft music playing. Ashara washed Aishah's hair and playfully pushed her under the water. Aishah came up sputtering and laughing and pulled Ashara down with her.

Serving girls held towels as they climbed out and dried each other. They shared the wine, figs, bread, and olive oil that were placed on a table in their room. Exhausted, Aishah eventually fell face down on the bed and went to sleep.

Late in the evening there were gentle bells and chimes ringing just as Ashara come into the room. Aishah awakened, looked around, and tried to orient herself.

"Tell me I am here, Ashara! I have dreamed it so many times."

She got up, dipped her hands into a bowl of water and washed her face. They sat down for an evening meal in a garden area where they could be alone.

"The journey was so long and many things happened. I want to tell you all about them."

She talked about when she was Jezebel and when she was Aishah and how they intertwined at times. She told Ashara about the High Priestess of Ishtar in Assur who welcomed her. Then how she returned on the journey back when Aishah was needed to help the High Priestess heal from an illness.

Ashara smiled her knowing smile.

"And there is something you are not telling me, Aishah. I can always sense it."

Jezebel stopped and took a deep breath.

"How can I tell you Princess Jezebel fell in love with the son of a stable owner? He was strong, handsome, and heroic! When I was kidnapped he used his own Arabian stallions to ride with Eser from Ebla to Ugarit to find me."

"It sounds like you could not help yourself! How could you not love him? He is your hero!"

"We gave the horses and pack animals to him as a gift before we left. It was so hard to walk away from him and board the ship. I still see him standing on the dock in Ugarit. Every part of me wanted to run back and ride away with him."

Tears began to spill over and she quickly wiped them away.

"You were Princess Jezebel who knew what her role in life had to be.

You were battling with Aishah, your heart and soul. Princess Jezebel had to win whether she wanted to or not."

"What have I done to Aishah? How will I get back my inner spirit?"

"She will not disappear. She is still there. She will be there through all the years of your life. Princess Jezebel must learn to call upon Aishah for support and see her as an equal partner."

"It is so hard to understand. Perhaps the heart is far stronger than I thought."

"Do not struggle with this, Aishah. Just trust the whole of you, all parts working together as one."

Chapter 25

The next day Aishah spent most of the time in the garden listening to the bells blowing in the breezes and letting everything within her settle into some peaceful place in her mind.

The following day Ashara started to take Aishah through the lessons to refresh them in her mind and anchor them in her soul.

After several weeks, a message came from King Ethbaal, requesting Jezebel return to Sidon.

Come home, my dear. It has been ever so long since I have seen you. I have a new adventure for you. I have rebuilt the town of Botrys and built a new one, Auza. I need you to administer governments at Botrys and Auza, to be a regent for me. Please come now.

Jezebel knew she must go. She kissed Ashara farewell and Hannibal procured a carriage to take her to the dock. The Phoenician ship was scheduled to leave soon. She had not been on a ship without Eser. She felt hollow and lost, and chanted over and over, *Aishah I need you. Be with me.*

When her ship docked in Sidon, Eser was there waiting for her. She ran down the gang plank to meet him. He caught her in his arms, kissed her, and they walked down the dock together to the carriage.

"What is happening here, Eser? Why are you not administering these small cities? Why me?"

"Jezebel, you are ready! I have some duties to take up in Father's government that will enable me to step into his place when I am needed. I cannot do that from small cities far away."

"What duties? What will you do?"

"We have alliances with Israel, Lebanon, and other places. Father needs an ambassador to speak for him in these places to keep the alliances strong."

"Oh, and I cannot do that?"

"Jezebel, you would bite their heads off and you now it. It is a study in keeping cool while negotiating whatever needs to be negotiated. Those small cities Father wants you to administer are important to Phoenicia. They are young and need a strong hand to govern and guide them. That is you!"

In the carriage Jezebel sat thinking most of the way to the palace.

"Where will I live?"

"You will live here at the palace and have officials in those cities to carry out your instructions. Father has selected some qualified men for you to interview. The choices of which ones will be up to you."

"I guess if I can learn to ride a camel, I can learn to do this, too. When do I start?"

"Father will meet with us tomorrow. He has taken the whole day off from his duties to spend with both of us. I am sure things will become clearer and less scary."

"I certainly hope so! I am so glad you will be there with me. I feel like my world has been jerked out from under me...again."

"The last time you said that, you were going to the School of Astarte. It turned out well, did it not?"

"Going to the school was like landing in the middle of soft pillows. This feels more like a bed of nettles."

They walked into the palace. The fragrances of a familiar place came to her first and settled Jezebel's jangled nerves a little. Her rooms were the same, beautifully prepared, and refreshments were on a side table. She was home but feeling alone, going from a world of love at the school to business and politics at the palace in Sidon.

Her dreams that night were filled with motion, the rocking of the ship and camels...and shadowy visions of Sikhar riding away. She tossed and turned most of the night and awakened in the early morning light feeling as if she had not slept at all.

She got up and walked to the window where the light was so bright it hurt her eyes. She wanted to throw herself back onto the bed and cry, as she had done so many years ago. Her father and Eser would be waiting to break their fast with her. And besides, it was childish.

Minah, her sweet elderly maid, came in to help her bathe and dress. A fragrant oil was rubbed into her hair and skin to help them recover from the constant exposure to sea spray, wind, and sun. A fresh tunic, jeweled girdle and sandals were laid out for her. As she put them on they felt stiff and unfamiliar after her loose flowing desert garments.

A sumptuous table of fruit, fish, vegetables, bread, and a hot drink awaited her as she joined Eser and her father. Ethbaal was a tall robust man with a huge beard. She could see he had many gray hairs reminding her of the aging of the cities she visited. Nothing was forever.

Eser greeted her warmly as they sat down together. Ethbaal said a short prayer to Astarte and cleared his throat.

"I am sure Eser has told you something about my plans for both of you. Your lives as royal power are about to begin. The incident of your abduction, Jezebel, was a beginning lesson on how dangerous the world is. And you were both wise to leave Nimrod when you did. Shalmaneser and his family are dangerous. Very dangerous. We may have to deal with them at some time in the future.

"You have seen empires rise and fall into ruins. You plotted the route of your return rather than coming back the same way in the caravan. That was good. I am so proud of you. I am also thankful you both came back unscathed and much wiser."

Eser was beaming and Jezebel did her best to keep an appreciative smile on her face. She could only listen but not offer anything further. Of course it was not a conversation. She would have an appropriate time to speak when the candidates for administrators of her cities were presented.

Ethbaal's receiving chamber was set up with tables and chairs covered with luxurious robes and cushions on a raised dais for the three of them. There were podiums on the lower floor from which the candidates could present their qualifications to Jezebel and answer her questions.

As they walked in and looked around, Jezebel whispered to Eser.

"I do not know what to ask. I will sound stupid."

"Just listen, my sister. Most likely our father will conduct the interviews himself. If you then have questions, you can speak. You might begin with 'how will you handle this situation or that problem' and again just listen and take notes.

"There will be a clay tablet and a stylus on the table in front of our chairs. You will look wise and discerning. Remember who you are, Princess Jezebel."

Chapter 26

K ing Ethbaal introduced everyone before the interviews began. Jezebel listened with her chin held high. She could feel the condescending looks and hear the patronizing words of the applicants when she was introduced as the administrator over both cities.

The first applicant addressed King Ethbaal. Jezebel looked up in surprise.

"Your Highness, are you sure it is not Prince Eser who is to be the administrator?"

A second applicant spoke up addressing the king.

"Your Highness, surely you do not expect us to work for a woman! I assumed it was you I would be reporting to since you called me here."

Enough was enough! It was time to assert her authority. She stood up and turned to her father.

"There is no point in continuing, Father. None of these are suitable. They are the kind who are smiling and agreeable to your face while going behind your back. They seem to think this woman knows nothing. She will be a push over and they will run things their own way."

She turned abruptly to the applicants.

"Not so! You are all dismissed!"

The applicants' mouths dropped in shock. They looked at King Ethbaal as if expecting him to put this outspoken woman in her place. He had qualified them!

"I said…you are all dismissed! Now go or I will have the guards throw you out."

They scurried out of the room and King Ethbaal broke into a roaring laugh, applauding loudly and continuing to laugh. Eser was applauding as well.

"It is true Jezebel, you are a woman and you will have to stand up against this sort of thing all your royal life. You have done well today, but we are not finished. I have two humble and worthy ones. The guards will escort them in immediately."

"Are you sure they are humble and worthy, my father, or is this another test?"

"See for yourself. Come in!"

Jezebel's mouth dropped open. They were Hannibal and Barek, her guards. She knew it was true. They were learned men who were humble and would have her best interests at heart as they always had.

"Yes! Of course! I am happy to accept them."

She smiled at Hannibal and Barek and they all broke into laughter. Servants brought in a special wine reserved for an auspicious occasion and they toasted their future together.

The three prepared to visit the new cities, which were rather like small towns. They would be a powerful team in administering them. Hannibal turned to Eser with a questioning look.

"Eser, we have heard little from you. Will you come with us? We could use your expertise in many areas."

"I do not wish to intrude. I know Jezebel can handle things well."

Jezebel smiled and turned to Eser.

"You have never intruded, Eser, except when you sneaked into my rooms to see what I was doing with my makeup and wigs."

"I was five."

"Please come with us. I will be without you in my life soon enough. Father will eventually marry me to royalty of another country and I might be far away."

"Yes, I will come with you this time if our father agrees."

King Ethbaal nodded his agreement and retired to his chambers to rest. Hannibal and Barek bowed politely and left the room.

Eser and Jezebel sat down to finish their wine and talk privately.

"Speaking of being married off, I believe Father has a bride in mind for me. I have heard him negotiating with someone from another city. I cannot say I am looking forward to a marriage, but it is his wish that I carry on the dynastic traditions. I must have a son to carry on after I leave this world."

"Or a daughter?"

"I knew you would say that. Yes…or a daughter."

Jezebel wanted to travel by horseback to Botrys, but since they needed time to talk on the journey, they opted for a carriage.

Their first destination, Botrys, was the rebuilt city on the sea coast. It had an enormous sea wall across the water front to hold the high tidal waves back.

A resident helped them find suitable quarters for a government building. It was not large, but as the city grew it could be enlarged. Barek and Eser selected officials to administer finances and marketing. Jezebel interviewed them briefly.

The approved officials gathered in a conference room to hear about the new government. Eser reminded them Princess Jezebel would be the royal administrator.

"Do you understand she is to be treated with respect and not to be dismissed because she is a woman? If there is any disrespect, there will be serious consequences. Are we all agreed?"

They all nodded in agreement and sat down to do the planning.

"Eser, I have never heard you speak so…um…forcefully! You are full of surprises."

"I know you thought I was a bit wimpy, but I really am not."

"I am sure no wimpy person could have stood me all these years."

Jezebel and Hannibal left Barek and Eser to finalize the work in Botrys and sailed to Auza, in Tunisia, the new city built by King Ethbaal. They sailed from Sidon traveling for several days to this far away region.

Auza was a pleasant surprise. Jezebel was delighted.

"This city looks clean and beautiful! It almost shines!"

Hannibal was smiling and pleased as well.

"Yes, the rebuilt city of Botrys was constructed on the old foundations and along the old narrow streets. But not this one."

They disembarked from the ship and began to walk through the streets close to the harbor. Hannibal stopped to inspect a few of the buildings.

"This new city is a marvel of the best engineering plans on fresh foundations, new wide streets, and beautifully designed buildings. I have not seen anything like it. I have seen many cities, but they were not new."

They were greeted by the principal administrators selected by the king when Auza was being built. They walked together to the government headquarters.

Hannibal and Jezebel spent some time interviewing them and making note of their answers. Jezebel was especially interested in how they received her questions, ideas, and suggestions.

Any hint of condescension would have been grounds for immediate dismissal. She was sure the king had admonished them about that. They treated her the same as they treated Hannibal, as if they were equal partners. It was refreshing. There was no tension and she felt she could breathe again.

The Inn of Ahinadab was ready to receive them. He was a long time Phoenician friend of King Ethbaal. In Sidon Ethbaal had met and chosen him to own and operate the inn.

A week later they sailed back to Sidon to compare experiences, notes, and plans with Barek and Eser. Jezebel's plan was to go back to Auza with Hannibal and live there for the winter months.

King Ethbaal was most interested to join their conversation. He turned to Jezebel upon hearing her plans.

"Can you not do your administering from Sidon? Those in Auza and Botrys will carry out your orders, I am sure."

Chapter 27

Aishah smiled through Jezebel at Hannibal and Barek. She realized how much she loved them.

"Botrys is not far and I am sure Barek will be able to handle all that needs to be done there. It is a similar culture and an old established city.

"But Auza is different. I do not understand why you built a city so far away, Father. It is an unfamiliar culture and I need to know more. I cannot do that in a short visit."

"I built it there for the exact reason you mentioned, Jezebel. It is a different culture, a different alliance, and a way to strengthen our trade route along the coast to keep Phoenicia strong. I will be sending Eser to Samaria, capital of Israel, to further those relations as well. Dangerous times are coming. I can feel it in my bones."

There was something about the way her father said *Samaria* that made Jezebel shiver. She could not imagine why he would want an alliance with backward countries like Israel and Judah.

She was thinking, *let them fight their own wars. Phoenicia is peaceful and has been that way for decades making it a wonderful place to live.*

Jezebel and Hannibal stayed in Sidon a few months longer to attend Eser's wedding. His bride was Syrian from Damascus. Her name was Laila, the third daughter of the king. Jezebel did not know whether to be happy for them or jealous someone was becoming more important than her in Eser's life.

Eser went to the docks with Jezebel and Hannibal as they were waiting to board the ship leaving for Auza. Laila did not come with him. She was shy, not able to speak the language well. Jezebel's poise, forthrightness, and power intimidated her.

Hannibal looked over the cargo on the dock allowing Jezebel and Eser to talk privately.

"Eser, what will happen while I am in Auza? What plans are in place for you and for me? What will you be doing?"

"I am guessing you will be administering Auza for a year or two, until Father believes you are sufficiently educated and adept at running the affairs of a city. I will be making diplomatic journeys to our allies and potential allies to increase trading relationships.

"It seems Assyria is becoming more warlike, building greater armies and preparing to attack. I know Father is determined not to be drawn into any military conflict. That is why he chose a bride for me from Syria. Heaven knows we never needed an army in Phoenicia. He is relying on negotiations and trade to keep us safe. I may become his chief negotiator."

"So, Auza is far enough away that there is no danger I will bite anyone's head off and start a war, is that right?"

"That is an interesting interpretation, my dear sister, but I do not think it is the reason. It might be a good place for you until he decides which marriage alliance would be the best for Phoenicia."

"Oh, how disgusting! I should have been traded off to Sikhar along with the horses!"

Hannibal returned to the gang plank when the captain signaled their departure and waited for Jezebel to come and board with him.

As she hesitated Eser wanted to reassure her.

"We can walk through our days now a few at a time and see what the future brings. I will send you messages when a ship is coming your way and you can reply on its return. We will stay close even though we are a long way from each other. Nothing can separate us."

She hugged and kissed Eser. She and Hannibal boarded the ship for Auza. As the rowers backed the vessel away from the dock and turned it toward the seaway, she stood on the deck and watched Sidon until it was a speck on the shore behind them.

Hannibal joined her and offered her a cup of wine. It was exactly what she needed.

"I saw your ship come into port. I thought it fitting I should greet you!"

"Seti! What are you doing so far from home…again? First you are in Byblos and now here."

"Yes, but it has been over a year since Byblos. Two or three years? I lose track."

"Please come to dinner with us. Hannibal and I are here as administrators of Auza, the city built by my father. Much as happened. We can catch up…"

Hannibal came off the ship after posting some messages for Eser and King Ethbaal. He and Seti greeted each other coolly. They went to the inn where Jezebel and Hannibal had secured permanent rooms and an administration office on their previous trip.

She told Seti about the caravan journey after a year at the School of Astarte. She spoke of Auza and corroborated details with Hannibal, indicating to Seti that Hannibal was no longer just her guard. He was now co-administrator with her of this city.

Seti could not shake his discomfort in Hannibal's presence. He had hoped see Jezebel alone. After all Hannibal was still an underling. They were royalty.

"Since Hannibal is here to do the administrative duties of Auza, perhaps you could visit me on my ship. We could sail to Rhacotis. Much has changed there."

"I am sorry, Seti, but my duties here will require all of my time throughout the winter months. Hannibal and I have much to do before we return to Sidon in the spring."

Clearly crestfallen Seti excused himself to go to his ship. Hannibal took a deep breath.

"Princess Jezebel, is there anything here I need to know about?"

"No, Hannibal. There is not. Seti is a lost prince, Egyptian royalty with no position, which leaves him wandering about with no particular purpose. Do not be concerned about his discomfort with you. He tried to brush Eser off when we were in Rhacotis several years ago. I warned him it was Eser he should get to know.

"He was just asking me to stay with him in Byblos when I signaled you and we left immediately to go to the School of Astarte. Be assured, Hannibal, I am always grateful for your presence, your appropriate attentiveness, and loyalty."

"Thank you, Princess. I am most grateful to be at your side."

Jezebel guessed Hannibal was in love with her and she loved him, too. But neither of them would ever take a step further and destroy all the blessings they shared just as things were.

They went into the city to gather information from various overseers about storage, supplies, equipment, buildings and maintenance. In their office at the inn they created plans for expansion of the city, its marketing capacities, and consulted the overseers again as to how they could be implemented.

The overseers were hesitant at first, but Jezebel and Hannibal were adept in overcoming barriers. It was clear they were co-administrators and quite knowledgeable. The overseers soon caught their enthusiasm and were eager to see the plans.

Changes would not come immediately. Jezebel could see it would take some time to get things rolling and insure their continuance. She needed the confidence of the overseers in her ability to grow the business of a city and partner with her.

Chapter 28

The overseer of the supplies and storage, Nazim, did not come to the planning meeting feigning illness. He was most unhappy and argued with everything Jezebel said. He refused to allow them to inspect storage areas and supply levels or even tell them where they were being kept.

"This is my city! I have always been trusted here. You cannot just come here and accuse me!"

"We have not accused you of anything yet. Princess Jezebel has asked you to see these areas for our records. King Ethbaal has given her the task of administering everything in this city and I am her on-site administrator."

"I will not take orders from a woman!"

Jezebel began glowering at the man and stepped forward.

"You will leave this city immediately! No overseer can ignore me or speak in a disrespectful way to me and stay."

"Leave? But I cannot! This is my home."

Hannibal took the man by the arm and guided him to the street. He yanked his arm away and stalked down the street waving his fists and shouting.

"Was I too abrupt, Hannibal? What should I have done?"

"His face has been closed like a fist and he has been grumbling to everyone even before you came. You did the only thing you could. Others have indicated there is something wrong with the supply levels. They have not been able to get what they need. They think he is selling them for his own profit."

After much searching and inquiring among the residents they found the storage places, some hidden underground and some in caves near the city. Hannibal engaged a young man named Hamid to oversee the removal of the supplies from these places and bring them to a new warehouse a few blocks from the harbor. Hamid's friends brought carts and wagons and worked diligently to transfer everything. Jezebel rewarded them generously.

"What shall we do about Nazim?"

They went to his house and found it empty. Neighbors said there was much shouting and screaming. He dragged his wife and her mother into the hills. They feared for the women.

"Now I feel sad for his wife and her mother. Surely they did not deserve to lose their home!"

As they walked toward the foothills of the Aures mountains they heard screams of a woman. They ran toward the screams and found Nazim with a knife in his heart. His wife and her mother spattered with blood.

Jezebel put her arm around the elderly mother who was about to fall down. The wife was on her knees keening and wailing.

"What has happened, old mother?"

"He wanted to kill us and came at us in a drunken rage with the knife. Then he tripped and fell on it."

Jezebel continued to hold the old woman in her arms while Hannibal helped the wife up. They took the women back to their home at the edge of the city.

"This is your home and you may keep it. We will help you with food and all you need. Do not be afraid."

They entered the house and saw that the furniture and crockery were broken and scattered about. Jezebel picked up a broom and began to sweep the dust and pieces out of the back door. Hannibal picked up the furniture and repaired what he could. It was clear Nazim took his rage out on his family and home.

Neighbors came in to help. They were relieved Nazim was gone. They brought new crockery and coverings. Jezebel greeted them all with love and hugs. Clearly Aishah was in charge today.

Jezebel and Hannibal set up their daily routines going about the city, connecting with people, and checking with overseers. Hannibal watched the financial accounting and shipping on the docks, and there were no more incidents.

At times they rented horses at a stable and rode high into the foothills where they could talk as they looked out over the city and coastline.

Messages came on ships from Eser. Laila was pregnant and Eser was busy traveling for the king. Jezebel sent messages back about the city and how much she missed him.

When spring approached Jezebel and Hannibal got ready to return to Sidon.

"I will come with you to Sidon. We will give our reports to your father. If he wishes me to continue, I will return to Auza."

"Of course he will want you to continue at Auza! What would change that?"

"I take nothing for granted, Princess. I will offer your father a choice, as always."

Jezebel felt disoriented again. She could not shake the feeling that at any moment everything could change and all would be taken away from her.

"I am torn! I want to stay here and yet I miss my home. Perhaps Laila will welcome my company. I am sure she will need a woman to be with her other than servants. At least I hope she will."

Jezebel had the feeling Eser was keeping something from her and she dreaded to think of what it might be. As eager as she was to return to Sidon, there was nothing there she could be excited about but being with Eser and the hope of a friendship with Laila

Hannibal will go back to Auza. Eser will be traveling and Laila might still be afraid of me. Perhaps Aishah will be able to connect with Laila and at least support her through the birth of her child.

Jezebel sadly bid farewell to the beautiful city of Auza and boarded the ship with Hannibal. She stood in the back of the ship to watch the sail away and the receding coastline. At the pull of the oars the vessel surged forward under her hands and feet. It felt like the way her life was going, suddenly surging and carrying her away.

Turning again toward the Great Sea, it seemed like the dark unknown was opening to swallow her. For a long time she held tightly to a rope that came down from the sails and fed into a pulley on the surface of the deck.

Hannibal brought her a cup of wine and stood with her.

"Will you come back to Auza soon? At all?"

"I will unless my father has other plans. More and more I am feeling my life is no longer my own. It may have been an illusion anyway. Until now I felt as if I were going toward something. Now I feel like I am being drawn down into an abyss."

"That must be frightening! Tell me more if you care to."

"My future and inevitable marriage is in my father's hands. I have not focused upon it before now. Until now there was much time before me and certain goals to be reached. But that will change soon. Something is closing in on me. I will ask my father if I might return to Byblos for a time. I hope he will grant me a reprieve."

"Perhaps I can sail with you to Byblos before I return to Auza. I fear we may be separated forever, once I return."

Chapter 29

"I have no say over what my life will become. It feels like the darkness closing in on me. I want to go to the School of Astarte to regain the inner freedom of Aishah and anchor in my mind and heart in it again."

Hannibal slipped his arm around her momentarily, then turned and walked to the bow of the ship. Jezebel closed her eyes against the tears that threatened to spill over. She swallowed the remainder of the wine and went to the cabin to lie down. The ship stopped for the night in Gaza and then continued up the coast to Tyre and Sidon.

Eser met her on the dock and held his arms out to her. It was such a relief he was there and she ran to him.

"Father sends you a message. You may continue to Byblos. He will send a message there when he needs you return home."

"Thanks to great Astarte! Do you know for how long?"

"No, but I am sure it will be a good length of time so you can become... adjusted."

"Adjusted to what?"

"You ask more questions than I have answers for. Just be happy, Aishah."

She smiled at his use of that name, hugged him, and kissed his cheek.

"I always miss you when we are not together, always."

She turned and re-boarded the ship. Hannibal waited on the deck and waved to Eser.

"Who will return with you to keep you safe, Jezebel?"

"I am sure Eser will come for me. Or Father will send someone if he is not there. Do not worry, Hannibal. You know firsthand I can take care of self. I will send a message to Auza when a ship goes there."

To Hannibal the trip to Byblos seemed short. Jezebel stood in the bow of the ship wishing away every nautical mile, eager to get there before something happened to snatch it all away.

It was evening when they disembarked and Hannibal called for a carriage to take them to the school. He left her at the gate as Ashara came out to meet her. His mind was filled with sadness and confusion as he returned to the ship. *How can I go on and do this without her? Yet it must be.*

"Aishah! What a wonderful surprise! Come in!"

They threw their arms around each other, laughed and wept.

"I thought we would never see you again and here you are. Is all well?"

"Let us go in and I will tell you all about everything."

After a relaxing bath and oil rubdown, they sat in their room wrapped in soft robes and Aishah told her the whole story, including losing herself in the dark abyss of an unsure future.

"Aishah, no matter how dark you think things might be, remember the light is within you. You have long been in the world of Jezebel, learning to administer a city. Even so you must maintain your vibration at the high rate of your spiritual nature. Darkness cannot overcome the light. It cannot snuff out a single candle.

"It was so good you remembered and comforted the old woman in Auza. Do you see how powerful that is? All the darkness of that day disappeared into the light of love. Even their neighbors were attracted to love. They came to help, bring gifts, and express their own loving nature."

The young priestesses brought them dinner in their room and quietly retired. Ashara and Aishah ate together, talking for a long time. Overcome with fatigue Aishah finally collapsed on the bed and slept.

When the morning light crept into the room, Aishah opened her eyes and closed them again. She thought being at the school was just a dream, but to her joy it was real. She was there again.

Ashara came in happy to see she was awake.

"If you are willing, I would like to review the advanced lessons of our year together. It will implant them deeper into your psyche, your consciousness of your spiritual nature. It will strengthen your confidence. It is not unusual to need another practice."

"I would love to do that! Anything to get rid of this dreading in the pit of my stomach."

Ashara and Aishah spent the next four weeks studying and practicing. Then there was a message from King Ethbaal. Aishah already knew what the message would be, a summons to return.

"Aishah, do not let the dark feeling come back. Do not let the dread come back. Change the vibration to light right now!"

"I am Aishah forever and this message will never change that. I look at everything through the divine light of Truth because I am light!

"I must return on the next ship coming from Sidon. It will be here in a week. Eser will be on it to travel back with me, thank blessed Astarte!"

"And bless Astarte we have another week together. Let us walk through Byblos together. There is another temple, a palace, and a few sacred places to visit. We can arrange an escort. It will be good to go into the world and experience it together before you must return to Sidon."

As they wandered through market places, gardens, and holy places, Ashara often asked Aishah what she was thinking. It helped her keep her consciousness high. It helped her feel what it is like to maintain her inner connection outside of the school, interacting with people in the markets and other places.

They went to the docks where the ships were coming in and out. The smells and shouts were rooted in her from her childhood. She practiced experiencing them as Aishah.

"Are Jezebel and Aishah together as one, now? Can you experience the outer and still be Aishah?"

"Yes, it is getting easier. Thank you for all your hard work and devotion to my training. I love you so much!"

Jezebel stood still in shock. Eser was coming down the dock toward them. Then she ran into his arms.

"But I thought it would be another week!"

"Yes, it will be another week before our ship returns. I wanted to come early and spend a little time with you."

Jezebel reached for Ashara and drew her forward.

"This is Ashara, my dear friend and trainer."

"The invitation includes Ashara, of course. Perhaps we can spend the time together. I can learn some of what Ashara teaches. My priestly training was different, more political than spiritual."

Ashara beamed.

"I would love to share the teachings with you! Were you given a spiritual name?"

"Yes, I was. It is my grandfather's name, High Priest Ahiram. He was a priest of Astarte and I am told his spirit now lives in me."

"Wonderful! We will begin when you are ready."

Chapter 30

Ashara continued to use Eser's spiritual name, Ahiram. The three of them talked for hours as they walked around Byblos. Aishah could not have been happier. On their way back to the inn Eser needed to stop by the dock to check for any messages.

There was a message from the captain of the Phoenician ship. There were storms on the Great Sea and the ship would be delayed another week for repairs to the sails.

Aishah wanted to jump for joy.

"Another week! Thank you, Astarte! Even though you are not goddess of the sea and storms, you must have some influence with the other gods!"

They settled into the guest building near the School of Astarte. Eser had been staying there and knew there was a meeting room that would serve as a classroom. Ashara began with the first lessons to be sure Eser, or the High Priest Ahiram, would not miss any of the elements.

Aishah spent some time in the temple taking on Ashara's duties there. Then the three would get together for dinner and evening walks.

Aishah noticed something different in their relationships. She did not feel left out, but a bond was forming between Eser and Ashara that looked familiar. It seemed to her they were falling in love.

"Eser, you know this can come to nothing more. Soon we will all be separated. Our lives and choices will not be our own. Have you and Ashara talked about this?"

"No. It is always about the lessons, which are miraculous! I love every minute of what I am learning. I guess I thought we would leave in another week and that would be a natural ending."

"And what about Ashara? Does she not deserve to be included in this discussion?"

"How will that change anything?"

"She is our friend, teacher, and she loves us. You cannot just drop her! She is part of us. Her feelings matter too."

Eser promised he would speak with Ashara even though it seemed pointless. Everything would come out the same anyway. But it was Ashara who initiated the conversation.

"I am not blind High Priest Ahiram. I know our love has deepened and there is no earthly place for it to flourish. But there is the cosmic place where it came from and will continue to reside. We must honor that love, not with emotions or plans to meet in secret, but with the Truth that love is as eternal as life itself. I know Aishah has met this lesson as well. These are loves we will carry in our hearts and always lift up to the Highest Heaven."

Eser was amazed and somewhat relieved Ashara spoke of it so eloquently. He still did not know what to say or what words to use. In all he was learning about the cosmic realm, this would be the most difficult lesson, to lift up what was so strong. It was demanding to be met at the lower vibrations of human life. He went out into the city to be alone while Aishah and Ashara went into the temple to complete duties.

"How do you think Eser is taking this? There has been so much to teach him, things that it took me a year to embody."

"Do not worry, Aishah, he is smart and strong. He will figure it out for himself, just as you have had to do. I know you wanted to stay with Sikhar and hide in Auza with Hannibal, but all of that would come to disaster. You must follow your destiny wherever it leads and so must he."

Dinner together was quiet. Their conversation drifted into long silences. Soon the wine took hold and relaxed them so they could laugh and easily discuss important things. They planned the last few lessons to fit into the time left. They shared their thoughts about where their lives would take them.

"Eser, do you know what Father has planned for me? You do know, do you not?"

"Father has sworn me not to tell you until he can talk to you when we get back to Sidon."

"Oh, Eser, how can we live with secrets? You have never kept anything from me. Please! I will pretend to be surprised or aghast, whatever is required. I am sure it is not wonderful news or you would have been bubbling to tell me."

"Father made me promise. Of course I could not refuse him. What could I say?"

"Eser, in the name of all we have meant to each other through growing up together and all our travels, please tell me now. Please!"

Eser, his face contorted with indecision, glanced at Ashara.

"Have you some wisdom that would help us?"

"It is a cruel promise. Your father will live out his days as he always has, alone and as the king. But you two are bound together, a bond more precious than anything else. You must decide which is most important. Which relationship must you have for your lives going forward?"

"I will let you know what I decide tomorrow."

"Tonight, Eser my beloved brother. Tonight...or I will not sleep!"

Eser sat without speaking for a little while. Then he took a deep breath and began.

"All right. I have been spending time in Israel with King Omri. Father wishes to forge stronger ties with him to keep our coastal cities protected. They are bordered by Samaria, where Omri's capital of Israel is located. From there he rules Judea which gives him more territory and power.

"Father believes a marriage alliance with Israel is the best way to keep Phoenicia safe from other kings who would think of invading us to take our seaports."

"Marry King Omri, that old man? Is he still alive?"

"No, he just died. You will marry his son, Ahab, who is succeeding him to the throne."

"And have you met this...prince?"

"Yes. He is amiable but not strong. He needs a strong wife to share the throne. Father believes you are that strong wife. Soon you would become queen, share the throne, and rule for the good of all."

Jezebel sat up straight. Israel was her worse nightmare. It was the place she least wanted to go.

"From what you have told me, Israel is a backward, xenophobic population, stuck in their religion and ready to go to war for it. That is why there is always a war of some kind going on there. I understand their god demands absolute obedience and punishes the so called sinners who refuse to obey.

"There is nothing good to recommend that place, Eser! It holds nothing for me. I will die there."

Eser and Ashara were quiet and just sat beside her as it all sank in.

"I am to be thrown away, buried in a place like Israel. Surely I deserve better. But of course it is not about me, but about political alliances and power. It is about... destiny."

Chapter 31

"Wait Jezebel. There are agreements to be made about what powers you will have. You will not be a servant wife, but a princess, a queen, knowledgeable and educated. Listen to Father. Start thinking of how you might negotiate to get that power for yourself. You are not helpless. You never have been."

"Thank you for telling me, Eser. I will not give up. I will negotiate and my demands will be many. Let Israel quake at the power of Jezebel."

"Let Israel quake at the power of Aishah! Remember where your true power lies. It is in your heart and spirit of Aishah. Any attempt at temporal power will weaken you."

"You are right, Ashara. It will be the biggest test in remembering who I am. Eser, do you know more about his father, King Omri? Was he a warrior or a peace maker, invader, power grabber? You have been there and met these people, have you not?"

"Yes. There have been years of constant civil war over the throne in Samaria and unsuccessful negotiations of peace with the Kingdom of Judah to the south. Israel has ten of the twelve tribes and Judah has two. But Judah has Jerusalem, the holy city, fortified and strong. They have the centerpiece of the Hebrew religion, the Ten Commandments, and history of Moses and Joshua. Those two tribes, Benjamin and Judah, stay together as one.

"Israel has no claim to the central power of Jerusalem. Samaria is a mixed race people, outsiders, and are not pure Jews. The ten tribes battle each other for territory and power which makes Israel unstable as a nation. This is what you will be walking into my beloved sister."

All of this was new to Ashara as well as Jezebel and more than a little frightening.

"But where can I do any good? What good will it do for me to be in the midst of constant wars? How does one govern such a country? I cannot think of anything in my experience that prepares me for this!"

Eser stopped for a minute to organize what he was about to say. He took Jezebel's hand and moved closer to her.

"Cooperation between the two rival states of Israel and Judah, plus relations with Tyre and Sidon to the north would be strengthened by a marriage between the two royal courts. You and King Ahab will be that marriage. A state of peace with Judah enables Israel to expand its influence and bring economic prosperity to the kingdom."

"But you mentioned war, not peace."

"Do you remember the warning we received from the mysterious man in Nimrod after we met Shalmaneser?"

"Yes, of course."

Jezebel turned to Ashara.

"An unknown man came to our inn to warn us we might be in danger. We stayed calm and made a plan. We would wait another day and leave unnoticed out of a side gate. When we got outside of the city, Hannibal and Barek had the horses and pack animals ready. We rode away unpursued. We must have been small fish in his greater plan to take Phoenicia."

Eser nodded and continued.

"It told us eventually Shalmaneser will come for us, threatening to expand Assyria toward the Great Sea and down the coast of Phoenicia. Plans were being made even when we were there. We have that mysterious man to thank for our safety if not our lives.

"Also the Kingdom of Aram has its palace in Damascus of Syria. King Ben-hadad is rising in power and threatening everyone around him. Israel will soon find itself at war in the northeast."

"Eser, we have lived in a world of peace and relative safety. Phoenicia does not have a military, even a small one. This is so hard to believe we are being thrust into a world of danger and war. It is hard to imagine this can happen to us!"

"Israel has a powerful army. They will protect Phoenicia in an attack if there is an alliance. An attack on Phoenicia would be an attack on Israel. Phoenicia has always negotiated its way out of trouble, even if it cost dearly. That is no longer possible. Everyone around us is too strong."

Jezebel was nearly in tears.

"I wish we could all go to Auza in Tunisia with Hannibal and stay there. Shalmaneser would not care to attack Tunisia. Too far away and there is nothing there he would want."

Ashara listened to this conversation with her eyes closed and then with her hands folded she turned to them.

"That sounds wonderful, but it is not your destiny. All you have learned has brought you to this moment and this time. Whether it is war or peace, prosperity or poverty, danger or safety, life or death, you will walk through it all as who you truly are and nothing need cause you to fear."

The ship arrived and they bid farewell to Ashara and the priestesses at the school. Ashara loved them so much and was sure she would never see them again. Tears streamed down her cheeks as the oarsmen backed the ship away and turned it toward the open sea.

After they boarded the ship Eser and Jezebel settled in and got to work immediately. Jezebel was listing her negotiating points and he was helping her think of what some of those would be.

"The big one will be keeping my religion and requiring altars to Baal and Asherah poles to Astarte to be erected near the Canaanite religious sites throughout Samaria.

"I want two personal servants, a scribe, and large private residential rooms in the palace. I will retain my title of Princess until Ahab officially becomes king. Then I will be Queen Jezebel, retaining all royal financing, dowry, privileges, and wedding gifts from foreign royalty.

"I will be free to move about the kingdom with a royal guard accompanying me at all times. I will be free to return to Sidon and Tyre from time to time to visit my family. I expect to be involved in governing decisions and be the only wife and consort of King Ahab."

"Very good! I will carry your demands to them in a diplomatic pouch and present them on my next ambassadorial trip to Samaria."

King Ethbaal met them at the dock in Tyre. They went to an inn for dinner and conversation. She handed the list of her demands to him.

He looked over her list and complimented her on knowing what she wanted.

"You deserve it all, my dear daughter. You are the principal figure in the alliance between the kingdoms. You show courage right from the beginning. That is good!"

"How long will the negotiations take? Am I to just sit here and wait?"

"What would you like to do, Jezebel?"

"I would like to go back to Auza since I am its royal administrator and confer with Hannibal on how our plans are progressing. You can send me word there."

"Excellent idea! You may return to Auza and see all is as good there as the reports sent to me. I trust Hannibal, but that is still your job to oversee everything. So go with my blessing. The Great Sea is quiet and a ship will be ready tomorrow."

"Thank you, father!"

Jezebel quietly thanked Astarte. It was one more reprieve from the looming unknown that cast a cloud over her life. It was another good thing to look forward to. She could hardly wait for the morning when she would board the ship.

Chapter 32

A special guard was not necessary on this trip because it was always the same ship's captain on her voyages. He knew her well and could serve ably as her guard.

Eser saw her to the docks. They parted as they always had with hugs and kisses.

"I know you were only half joking when you said you wanted us to hide out in Auza forever. Be sure to come back, Jezebel..."

They both broke into laughter and hugged again. He boarded the ship with her, greeted the captain, and then went back to the dock. A shout could be heard to signal the rowers and they backed the ship away from the dock.

Eser waited until the ship was in the channel and the sails were raised. Then he went back to the palace a little sad, but knowing he had a big job to do for her. She trusted him with her life.

The winds on the Great Sea were not favorable which slowed the progress of the ship so Jezebel spent extra days on the sea getting to Auza. She had left her list of negotiations in Tyre. She wanted no reminders of what was coming. One more time she wanted to experience the freedom of being on her own. The longer the negotiations took, the more precious time she had to herself.

She sat on the deck with the wind in her face and hair. At times she would help the crew do some tasks she could manage. She asked them about their families and lives, how many children they had and who their parents were. It kept her focused on the here and now, letting Aishah do her work of reminding her to love and be at peace with the whole universe.

Hannibal was amazed to see her get off the ship after he left her at Byblos a few months ago. He expected never to see her again. But here she was and he was overjoyed.

"Jezebel! You are always surprising me!"

"You look different, Hannibal. What is happening? Are you well?"

"Yes, I am well. How is it you have come here? Has something happened?

"There is a lull in the negotiations about my future. I decided to wait it out here and be happy a little longer."

"I am glad you have come. You can celebrate with me. I have decided to marry now that your life is taking you away. Our destinies are parting us and a marriage will be good for me. I am not getting any younger. The comforts of a home and family are calling."

"Hannibal, that is wonderful! Of course I am jealous! You have made a choice for your life, but mine is being made for me even now. Who is she? When will I meet her?"

"You already know her. She is the widow of Nazim, the woman whose abusive husband fell on his own knife. I am sure you remember the scene we came upon. Almost impossible to forget.

"Anah and her mother, Juha, have made me most welcome in their home and lives. Come with me. They will be happy to see you. You were so tender and caring about them. They have never forgotten it."

They walked to the inn to deposit Jezebel's belongings and then started for the house at the edge of the city.

Anah opened the door, squealed with delight, and ran into Jezebel's arms. She was not the bedraggled, blood smeared woman Jezebel had seen before, but now a lovely woman with a bright smile and shiny amber hair.

Mother Juha came out of the door behind her and ran to Jezebel, too. She looked much younger than Jezebel remembered. *Hard times always age one, but happiness has brought back youth for both of them.*

They pulled her into the house, which was different as well. Not a broken down shack but a reconstructed, enlarged, and sturdy dwelling with large windows to let in the breezes and fluttering curtains.

She looked back at Hannibal who was beaming with pride. She could not help but smile back at him. He looked younger too.

"It is beautiful, Hannibal. They look wonderful. You have done well for yourself and for them. My jealousy has turned into admiration and love for all of you. Blessings of Astarte to you."

"Jezebel, you have lit up my life for all the years I had the good fortune to be a guard and traveling companion for you and Eser. It is my hope someone will guard you all the days of your life since I cannot."

"As far as I know, I am still the royal administrator of this city and I will watch over you now! I am returning the favor."

Jezebel and Hannibal spent their days going through the city from end to end and storehouse to storehouse, cataloging and checking records. She insisted upon staying at the inn rather than with Hannibal's future family as they wanted her to.

One evening Anah and Juha came to see Jezebel at the inn. She was delighted and puzzled.

"Princess Jezebel, it has been told to us as a royal person you can perform a marriage ceremony for Hannibal and me. Hannibal sent us to ask you so you would not feel pressured in any way. Would you be willing to do that? Will you marry us?"

Jezebel's mouth dropped open. She never could have imagined this as one of her royal duties.

"I have never done such a thing. I am not sure I know how."

"It is not difficult. You just pronounce us husband and wife in the name of the crown and we will sign a document."

"Surely there must be more to it than just that. You and Hannibal deserve so much better. Let me think upon what we can do to celebrate. I will talk to you and Hannibal tomorrow."

Anah dropped the formal "Princess" and threw her arms around Jezebel.

"Oh, thank you! Thank you, my sister! We will see you tomorrow. Hannibal will be pleased."

Jezebel had doubts that Hannibal knew about this, but she would see tomorrow. *Hannibal…will be…pleased? I hope so!*

"Jezebel, do you think there is anything around here I do not know about? I can even read faces and know what is happening. Yes, I am pleased!"

She picked out a place on a deserted dock so they would be next to the sea and its cooling breezes. A resident gave her some flowers and a pot for them. A shop gave her a length of metallic gold and blue woven material. As she gathered items, she invited the residents to attend as well.

When all was in place, she led Anah and Juha out onto the dock. She placed the gold and blue material over Anah's head and anchored it with a crown of flowers and ribbons. She gave Juha a small bouquet of flowers to hold. Hannibal arrived in a new tunic and sandals. He brought a gift of rings for Anah and a bracelet for Juha. Residents began to file onto the dock with flowers and small gifts, singing a song of joy.

Jezebel read a poem about love and had them recite after her some gentle vows and blessings for their future.

"Do you accept each other as husband and wife?"

"Yes, we do!"

"Then in the name of the royal crown of Phoenicia I decree you are married."

The residents cheered, danced, and wished them well as they exited the dock. Anah, Juha, and Hannibal were in tears, so touched by it all.

There was a banquet at the inn open to all those who attended. It lasted far into the night. They toasted each other over and over, and eventually all fell asleep on the upholstered benches and carpeted floor.

Chapter 33

The sun rose on a new day and people with bleary eyes and hangovers. But they were happy, especially Hannibal and Anah. They gathered their gifts and Jezebel gave them the papyrus with the poem and their vows written on it. The innkeeper loaned them a small pull cart to carry their gifts and flowers home.

Jezebel remained at the inn. She was exhausted and happy for the couple. She refused to allow Jezebel to envy them but rejoiced as Aishah in all the love and happiness.

Two days later Hannibal brought two horses around to the inn and invited Jezebel to ride with him along the sandy beaches and up into the foothills. A good stopping place was on a small bluff overlooking the sea. They sat down on a rock and reminisced about all their travels and experiences, and how it all came together in this day and time.

"Jezebel, what are your thoughts about your future? Do you fear it? Shall we go back and find Sikhar?"

Jezebel laughed and slipped an arm around him.

"Only you and Eser would say something like that to me. Of course Eser would not say it now because he is afraid I would actually do it! Eser's description of King Ahab is not reassuring."

She heard Aishah say, *there is nothing good to come from fearing.*

"What description is that? What did he say?"

Jezebel squinted her eyes and pushed her hair back from her face.

"He is not strong although not unpleasant to look at. His kingdom is constantly at war with someone and their kings murder each other every week. I gave my father a list of negotiations, demands if you will. Eser has taken them to Samaria. I do not know how long negotiations take, but I know Eser will not let me down. He will insist everything on the list be honored."

"What demands did you require? Do you mind telling me?"

She listed them for Hannibal as best she remembered them.

"Jezebel, I am troubled by the danger you might be in. Is there anything I can do? Any way to help you?"

"No Hannibal. Just knowing you are here, safe and happy is enough. Destiny is a hard task master. I cannot run away from it. Nor would I ruin Sikhar's life. He would be much happier with his horses."

"I will never believe that!"

"You know me. Believe it."

They rode back into the city and stopped at the inn where they had a few glasses of wine to wash away the dust from their throats. Then Hannibal left to return the horses to the stable and went about his business.

Jezebel climbed the stairs to her room, sat down, took out a sheet of papyrus, and began listing her demands as she remembered them. Then she sat in meditation, praying to Baal and Astarte to watch over her. She soon fell asleep in the heat of the late afternoon. When she awakened, Juha was sleeping beside her and a bowl of fruit was on the table.

"Juha! What are you doing here?"

"Oh, please forgive me! I brought you some fruit and your bed looked so soft I thought I would lay down on it for just a minute. And then I fell asleep. I am so sorry."

Jezebel laughed, got up and hugged Juha. They ate some of the fruit together and went down the stairs to the dining room.

"I must go home and help Anah. She will wonder what has happened to me!"

She hurried out the door and up the street toward home. Jezebel smiled at the thought of Juha laying down beside her and falling asleep. She was reminded of how Ashara and Aishah loved to fall asleep together.

Weeks went by and Jezebel slipped into a routine of visiting the businesses with Hannibal. She knew the owners, their families by their names, and spoke to them every day. It was a lovely time that might never come again.

She expected to be summoned home by her father at any time. When Eser arrived on the next ship Jezebel was so surprised. She ran to the dock to greet him.

"Eser, what has happened? Has something happened to Father?"

"No. I have come to talk with you in person, to share with you how the negotiations are going."

"Oh...and how are they going, my brother?"

"They have been trying to argue about everything. I remind them constantly you are royalty and must be treated as such."

"How strange! Why do you have to keep reminding them?"

"They send in different negotiators every time we begin to make progress. It is frustrating. I have to start all over with the new ones."

"What does Father say about this?"

"He said it is up to me."

"Good! Then you tell King Ahab and whoever else is involved, I will wait no longer. If they do not agree to everything I have asked for within one month, the wedding is off!"

Eser sat back on the bench in the inn dining room and laughed. Hannibal came in and Eser repeated Jezebel's vehement answer. All three burst forth in laughter.

"That is my Jezebel! Do not take anything less!"

"I will be valuable to their kingdom. I will not put up with their cowardly negotiators nor back away from my demands. Those demands are just. They should know that and be glad to honor them or I will not to go there! I am a princess, not a servant."

Eser wrote down exactly what Jezebel said, word for word, and she signed it.

"Since I am here I will stay for a while and you can show me around the city. And Hannibal, what is this I hear? You have married?"

"Yes, I have and your sister created a beautiful ceremony for us. My wife is the widow, Anah, whose abusive husband fell on this own knife in a drunken fit of rage and died."

Eser glanced at Jezebel to see her reaction. As long as he had known her, even though she smiled through almost everything, he could always tell what was behind her smile.

He sensed resignation. Hannibal had been with them both for so long, and the parting was bitter sweet. His marriage in some way made the parting final.

After touring the city and its resources for several days, Eser decided it was time to return to Sidon.

"I must deliver your response to Samaria and then go to Botrys to assist Barek. I do not think he needs my help, but Father will require a report of his progress soon."

"So soon? The longer you stay the longer I am free. What do you think Father will say?"

"I am sure Father will enjoy your response. He is aging and does not wish to engage in this tedious process. He is certain you and I will prevail without him."

"Indeed we will!"

Chapter 34

"Eser, tell me one thing I will like about Samaria, if there is anything."

"I have to think about this. There was not much I liked when I was there, including their Jewish religion. Their god is strict and punishing. I do not know why anyone would worship a god like that. Many of their people prefer the old Canaanite gods which are more like ours, gods of fertility and plenty."

"Is there nothing? I need something encouraging, dear brother, or on the voyage back to Sidon I shall jump into the Great Sea!"

"Jezebel, can you swim like the fish?"

"No and I do not intend to swim. Just sink!"

"All right. I have thought of something. Samaria and especially the palace is on a huge hill, so high you can see the twenty three miles to the Great Sea. You will always be able to see your beloved ships passing. Of course they will be tiny dark specks from so far away, but you will know they are there."

"That is all?"

"That is all. You asked me for one thing and I had to reach for that one."

She walked with him to the dock where his ship was waiting. She hugged him and kissed his cheek.

"Be strong and be well. My love and the blessings of Baal and Astarte go with you."

"And you my beloved sister."

Many weeks went by and she heard nothing from Eser. But a surprise visitor arrived.

"Seti! What are you doing here? Did your sailors mistakenly go past the port at Rhacotis?"

She hugged him and they laughed.

"I was coming back to Rhacotis and heard about Auza, and that you were here. So I decided to sail on to visit you and the city your father built. I hoped you would welcome me."

"Of course. Come. We will find you a room at the inn and then I will show you the city. But please do not mention you are *Prince* Seti, or people will think you have come here to take me away. They would not be happy about it and might attack you."

They sat in the dining room and talked over wine and bread.

"Actually, I hoped you would not only welcome me, but accept my proposal of marriage."

Jezebel's mouth dropped open. She had never considered Seti wanted anything more than a night in her bed, or a higher royal standing because of her.

"Seti, my dear that would be impossible. I am sorry. You see my father has negotiated a marriage for me with King Ahab of Israel. My brother is sorting out the details of a marriage contract as we speak."

Seti's shoulders sagged a little. He grew silent and gazed out of the window for a short time.

"I am sorry. I should have asked you when we were in Byblos. I should have approached your father even before then."

Jezebel looked out of the window, trying to think of what to say. Ashara had told her she had a destiny to fulfill, and she knew it was not with Seti.

"It would have made no difference. My father was planning a powerful alliance with Israel to protect Phoenicia. There is no army in Phoenicia, and no protection now that Shalmaneser is threatening war on surrounding territories. Israel has a strong military built by Ahab's father, King Omri, but weak governmental leadership. They need a regent while King Ahab is on the battle field, someone who can rule in his absence."

"But Egypt is not at war. We could share a peaceful existence floating on the Nile River, exploring pyramids and ancient cities, and sailing on the Great Sea to Carthage and other ports. You would have a nice life with me. Israel is a turbulent place. There is no peace there."

"That sounds lovely, Seti, but it is not for me. My destiny lies elsewhere, even in Israel if that is where it leads me."

"Then we shall speak no more of it. Please, show me your city and let us enjoy a time together."

Jezebel sent a young messenger to notify Hannibal of Seti's arrival and he came to join them. The three toured the growing city. Seti was not pleased to see Hannibal. He was just a guard in Byblos. How could he rise to be an administrator of this city with Jezebel!

Jealousy rose up in him like bile. He struggled to keep it at bay while they walked through the city. Hannibal sensed Seti's anger and jealousy. Nevertheless, he was attentive in giving Seti the tour as he would any other visitor.

Seti's ship would be sailing soon. He boarded it and turned his face toward the sea. His dreams of Jezebel faded with every flap of the sails.

A Phoenician ship pulled into port a few days after Seti left. King Ethbaal disembarked followed by his guard. Hannibal saw his ship arriving and hurried to meet him on the dock.

"Sire! What a pleasure to see you! Jezebel is in the market place assessing a way to enlarge it. Would you like to go to the inn to rest or would you prefer I take you to the market?"

"Ah, Hannibal! It is good to see you as well. Just take me to the market if you will. I can rest later if I need to. I am old but I prefer not to let it stop me."

Hannibal called for a carriage and drove King Ethbaal to the market place. Jezebel was working with an engineer on the layout of the market extension when she saw the carriage coming.

"That is my father!"

She ran toward the carriage calling out and waving. Hannibal stopped the carriage and Jezebel hopped in. She threw her arms around Ethbaal and kissed his cheek.

"Welcome to our city… yours, mine, and Hannibal's! May we show you around?"

"Yes, please do. It has been a long time since I have seen it, since I built it. I see my legacy continues and prospers!"

Hannibal stopped the carriage at a stand to get wine and cheese for the king to enjoy. They drove up and down streets, past the commercial district, and along the beach. Soon evening was upon them bringing a soft breeze from the sea and a beautiful sunset.

Back at the inn over dinner, King Ethbaal was preoccupied. He toyed with his food and gazed out of the window.

"Something is on your mind, Father? I am sure this is not just a pleasure voyage. What is it?"

"You and Hannibal are quite happy working together, are you?"

"Hannibal and I have always been happy working together. I must tell you his good news. He has married. Does that answer any other questions on your mind about us?"

"Forgive me, my daughter. I sent you and Hannibal here together and now I am taking you away. I do care how you feel about your life even though there are things that must be decided and may not be to your liking."

"I know, my father. You have given me all a daughter could ask for, education, travel, responsibility, and your blessing in all I have accomplished."

Chapter 35

"Well, one piece of joyful news is I have become a grandfather. Laila has had a boy child who will be Prince Mattan II. His father, your brother Baal Eser II, now lives in Tyre and will become the King of Tyre. Tyre is expanding far beyond Sidon in power and financial importance. Eser will need to rule from there."

"So I am Aunt Jezebel! How wonderful! I am so pleased for Eser and Laila. I hope she is well since the birth."

"And now to the other news."

Clearly King Ethbaal did not wish to carry the subject any further. Child birth was not something men cared to discuss.

"I need to bring you back with me shortly. We must begin your marriage ceremony plans to wed King Ahab and your transition to Samaria. King Ahab has agreed to all your demands and is eager to welcome you."

"Eser did a wonderful job taking care of my concerns, did he not?"

"Yes, and I think you will find King Ahab quite malleable and easy for you to share the rule. You will be Queen Jezebel and a powerful queen I am sure."

All of this settled upon Jezebel like a heavy mantle. Her life had changed over dinner. Her partnership with Hannibal would come to an end and a joyful partnership it was. She could depend upon Hannibal to share power with her, and be a solid rock for her to lean upon. Now that rock was being taken away and she felt a little unsteady.

King Ethbaal reached over and touched her arm.

"Do not worry, my daughter. Eser and I will not desert you. The welfare of Phoenicia depends upon you. We will be in contact with you often."

Jezebel closed her eyes for a moment and summoned Aishah into her consciousness. She placed her lost dreams deep in her heart for safe keeping.

"This alliance, as they put it, is my marriage and I hope it will be more than just a political one. I will do my best to make it so."

"What are you thinking Jezebel? You have not said much."

Her eyes fluttered open and she smiled at him.

"Please remember, my father, this is also a marriage between two people who will hopefully find comfort and happiness being together."

"Yes, well I am sure you and King Ahab will work that out. Tomorrow I would like to see more of the city and meet Hannibal's wife. I assume she is a local, not a foreigner, and will be as devoted to Auza as we are."

Jezebel was determined not to be derailed.

"Father, I did not know my mother or what your relationship was like. She died soon after Eser was born. Would you tell me about her? Did you...love each other?"

"Well, we produced you and Eser. Eser will follow me on the throne. I do not know what else I can tell you. I am a bit weary. I will go to my room and see you in the morning."

Jezebel swallowed the last of her wine hard, jolted at the sudden change of topic again as if she were prying. Disappointed, she also went to her room.

There was no one else in her life with whom she could speak to learn about marriage and what she should expect. She did not have aunts or cousins, and no friends who were married. This was a huge piece of her education that was missing.

Perhaps one more time I could prevail upon Hannibal to help me. But how will I even approach the subject?

In the morning Hannibal came for them with a carriage and Jezebel could see there would be no time to talk with him. Perhaps she could escape for a little while to speak with Anah and Juha. Still she was not sure what to ask them.

When they stopped at Hannibal's home, Anah and Juha came out to meet them. They looked a little frightened, but King Ethbaal was very gracious and put them at ease. Jezebel saw her chance and told Hannibal she needed to speak to Anah. She would catch up with them later. King Ethbaal looked a little perplexed, but Hannibal smiled as if he knew what this was about.

"Anah, I must leave with my father soon. A marriage has been arranged for me to King Ahab of Israel. I do not know much about marriage."

Anah knew exactly what Jezebel was feeling. Gently she took her hand and led her into the house. Juha poured some wine and they all sat down together. Anah was not hesitant to talk about marriage. They had a long conversation about almost everything and Jezebel was much relieved. She could sense Aishah's presence in her, strengthening and calming her.

"Thank you for sharing this with me. You are both my true sisters and I love you."

They all hugged and kissed each other and Jezebel left to find Hannibal and her father. That would be easy since it was the only carriage in the city fit for a king. Everyone would be outside waving and pointing in the direction it was going.

Then, instead, she decided to walk back to the inn by way of the docks, smell the sea air, watch the birds, and be alone with her thoughts.

"Can a queen also be a wife? Are they to be lovers? And if they should love each other, can they co-rule a kingdom? What would King Ahab be thinking about this? Father said he would welcome me. That sounds hopeful. Did he dismiss the negotiators who were delaying things so he could get on with the marriage and political alliance?

How did Eser bring this about so quickly? What did Eser tell him about me? What is he expecting? Eser, who is now a father, who has a throne awaiting him. My beloved brother. How fortunate I am to have a brother who is also my best friend. I would be lost and alone without him."

The ship was ready to sail and Jezebel said a tearful goodbye to Hannibal, Anah, and Juha. Nearly half of the city was there to see them off as she boarded with King Ethbaal. Jezebel walked to the stern, leaned on the rail, and watched until the city became a small speck and disappeared.

King Ethbaal came and stood beside her.

"You will miss them, will you not?"

"Yes, being alone in Samaria I will miss everyone I have known all my life. It feels like an abyss with no bottom in sight."

It was clear Ethbaal did not care to join a conversation about her feelings and as usual abruptly changed the subject.

"Eser brought your wedding plans back from Samaria. I have them with me. I thought we might go over them together. You can make whatever changes you think best."

They walked back to the small cabin and sat down together. Ethbaal laid out the papyrus on a small table and Jezebel tried to concentrate on the details.

"What was your wedding ceremony like, Father? Please tell me about it from beginning to the end of the celebration."

King Ethbaal sat back and pulled at his beard.

"Your mother was beautiful like you. I met her just before the ceremony."

"You saw her for the first time minutes before marrying her?"

"Yes, Jezebel. That is when you and King Ahab will see each other, just before the ceremony. There is no decision making even if one of you finds the other unacceptable on sight! Even then the ceremony will take place."

Chapter 36

"And if that happens, if they do not want to marry each other? What if one is imbecilic? What do the prospective bride or groom do? Just run away?"

"I do not know, Jezebel. I have never seen it happen. I am not marrying you to an imbecile. Please! You ask too many questions. If you want me to tell you about my wedding, you will have to remain quiet and let me speak."

"Yes, that is what Haman used to say to me. I will be quiet."

Ethbaal listed his preparations and ceremony item by item. Jezebel was amazed at how much there was to do behind the scenes.

"You will arrive at the palace and from that moment on servants will guide you, dress you, instruct you, and be sure everything is in perfect order. Your changes of clothes, robes, and jewels will be chosen for you. You will not need to do anything except say yes."

"Who will officiate at the ceremony? Will it be a priest?"

"No, it will be a government official holding high office. It cannot be a priest. There are so many religions there we would surely insult someone, or everyone. There are Jews, Canaanites, Assyrians, Moabites, and a myriad of others. You and King Ahab can choose to have a private blessing with a priest of Baal if you wish."

"Will you be there? You and Eser?"

"Yes, of course. Do not worry."

Eser and Laila came to meet them on the dock. Laila's personal servant carried the baby. Jezebel was awe struck. Eser took the baby from the servant and carried him to Jezebel and Ethbaal.

"Here, my sister, hold your nephew. His name is Mattan."

"But I have never held a baby. I am not sure how."

"Just hold out your arms and take him. You will be fine and so will he."

Jezebel glanced toward Laila who was standing behind Eser. She stepped forward and took the baby from Eser.

"Please, my sister Jezebel, you may hold him. It is wonderful to hold a baby."

Jezebel held out her arms and Laila placed the baby in them. Jezebel held him close and felt his weight and warmth. Large trusting eyes looked up at her and his little fist came out of the blanket and found his mouth.

"Oh, Laila, it is indeed wonderful to hold a baby. Thank you!"

She cuddled Mattan a little longer while Ethbaal and Eser turned aside to talk for a moment. When they were ready to go to the carriage, she handed him to the servant who was waiting anxiously to take him.

Laila turned to Jezebel again.

"Now when you have your own babies, you will know how to hold them. Mattan is my only child since my body will not produce another. The birth was difficult but I am so happy to have him."

Jezebel felt a rush of compassion and put her around Laila's shoulders.

"I regret we will have little time to get better acquainted, but let us use these few days to do just that."

Laila beamed and hugged Jezebel. They walked hand in hand to the carriage.

During the next week, Jezebel had another opportunity to talk with a married woman. Laila was willing to tell her about her ceremony and marriage. They treasured every moment knowing they must soon part when Jezebel must go to Samaria.

"I will not be at the wedding, my dear Jezebel, because my health will not permit the travel. It is taking longer to gather my strength than I hoped. I understand, Laila. Stay with dear little Mattan and get your strength back. Perhaps I can come to see you soon."

Before dawn carriages and wagons were packed, horses saddled, and all was in readiness to make the trip to Samaria. Jezebel wanted to ride a horse part of the way. They saddled one for when she wanted to get out of the carriage to see the countryside.

She hugged and kissed everyone, and got into the carriage with King Ethbaal and Eser.

"How far is Samaria, Eser?"

"It is about fifty miles. We will go down along the coast of Phoenicia and cross over into Galilee for a short distance. It borders on Samaria."

"Would you mind very much if I rode the horse through the countryside and into Samaria now? I would like to be alone."

"Stay close. Do not go running off."

"We are not in Ebla, Eser."

They gave each other a mischievous grin.

Jezebel rode through Galilee past Mount Carmel. It gave her more confidence to be riding. She was going on her own instead of being taken in a carriage.

When they got to the border of Samaria, Jezebel was surprised to see a royal entourage coming toward them. The carriages both stopped. Ethbaal and Eser got out to greet King Ahab.

She sat there frozen on her horse not knowing what to do. King Ahab came to the side of her horse and offered his assistance as she dismounted.

"I suppose someone should properly introduce us, Princess Jezebel. Of course I know who you are, but that is beside the point."

King Ethbaal stepped up to make a formal introduction. It was so elaborate Jezebel began to laugh. King Ahab looked from Ethbaal to Jezebel and began to laugh uproariously.

All of the tension went out of Jezebel as Ahab kissed her cheeks and they walked to his carriage. Ethbaal was soon nodding off in his carriage. Eser felt at loose ends after being the central person negotiating this marriage. With no one to talk to he decided riding the rest of the way on her horse might calm him.

In King Ahab's carriage Jezebel decided to get right to what was on her mind.

"You know I expect to be a full partner in this marriage and in the rule of Israel, do you not? My demands you signed will be honored. Do you agree with me?"

Ahab was wide eyed at the sudden change in conversation from what he thought it would be.

"Are you always this forthright in your manner, Princess Jezebel?"

"Yes, I am. My brother surely told you that. And you can tell by the things I asked for as conditions of our marriage I expect them to be fulfilled."

"Yes, well…tell me of your education, your experiences and travel, your oversight of the city of Auza. Eser has told me some things, but I would like to hear it from you. I am sure Solomon and all his wives did not meet one like you."

"I believe, King Ahab, the Queen of Sheba was quite Solomon's equal. Is it not the way your history tells it?"

"Indeed it is! So you know something of our history as well as Phoenicia and Mesopotamia. Tell me more about this relationship of which you speak."

"I am to be your wife, my king, and also your friend and ally. I will learn from you, support you in all you do, and protect you from your enemies. I will be of service, speak my mind respectfully, and gladly take part in whatever is within my expertise."

"This is interesting and unexpected. I find it most intriguing. I have not heard a woman speak as you do."

"Have I offended you, Sire?"

"No, not at all. I believe I am looking forward to an education!"

"As am I!"

Chapter 37

Jezebel was not sure she could trust his word as yet, but the relationship began to look promising. He was attentive, likeable, and intelligent.

"Please tell me about you, Sire?"

"Ahab, please. Call me Ahab when we are together.

"My father left me a huge kingdom to rule. He was a warrior all his life. He taught me battle strategies but not negotiation. He did not negotiate. He just took what he wanted. I learned to be a good warrior, but I cannot live up to his power or agree with his constant aggression against our neighbors.

"It seems good to live in peace if we are not threatened. From the look of things in Assyria, that may not be possible. Shalmaneser is an aggressor of the worst kind.

"I know little of being a husband, so perhaps we can learn about that relationship together."

It was late when they arrived in Samaria. The palace on the hill was brightly lit with torches. Jezebel was amazed at its size. The walls were high and seemed to go on forever. Huge ornate gates swung open for them and the courtyard was large enough to accommodate several camel caravans.

Immediately servants dashed out to meet them. Some began unhitching the horses and others escorting everyone to their quarters.

"Rest well, Princess. My people will take good care of you. I will see you tomorrow at the ceremony."

"And you, Ahab. Rest well."

The servants came into Jezebel's rooms early and began laying out clothing and jewelry everywhere. She looked at the array and wondered if she were supposed to wear all of it in one day. They bathed her, oiled her, dried her, oiled her again, washed her hair and arranged it to hold a crown. They helped her into undergarments that would support the wedding dress and sat her on a stool in front of a mirror to apply her makeup.

The servants were skilled in every phase of dressing her. Their efficiency was almost dizzying. A servant held the mirror before her to see their handiwork.

"There, my lady, you are beautiful!"

"Will I wear all of these different clothes today?"

"Oh yes, my lady. We will be ready for you at each part of the ceremony and throughout the day. We will escort you there and return you here. We will take off this gown and put another one on you, fix your hair, and touch up your makeup."

Jezebel smiled to herself wondering if they would also accompany her to Ahab's bedroom. She decided not to ask. What she was experiencing at the moment was enough.

The great hall was beautifully decorated and the officials, their ladies and guests awaited her arrival. A group of harpists were playing. King Ahab looked resplendent in all of his kingly vestments as he stood with the officiant on a raised dais.

As she entered the hall, Prince Eser and King Ethbaal stepped to either side of her. She took their arms and they accompanied her down the long aisle.

"Eser, did you and Laila go through all of this?"

"Yes. All of it."

"It must have exhausted Laila!"

"And me."

Ethbaal and Eser stepped away at one point and Jezebel continued forward alone. At the steps of the dais, Ahab stepped forward and offered his arm which she took, grateful for the physical support. The elaborate jeweled sandals they gave her were killing her feet.

"Are you all right, Princess?"

She smiled her most dazzling smile at Ahab.

"Yes, but my feet hurt. I think your servants did not realize how big my feet are."

They both began to laugh. The official before them kept a grim look and began the ceremony in a stern voice. Jezebel listened to every word to be sure nothing was said to which she would object.

When the official asked her if she took Ahab as her lord and master she smiled and replied so all could hear.

"I take Ahab as my husband and my equal."

And Ahab grinning replied in a booming voice.

"And I take Jezebel as my wife and my equal."

A loud murmur went through the whole room. The official's face turned red and the veins bulged in his neck. But Ahab and Jezebel stood their ground smiling at each other and the service came to a conclusion. There were cheers and applause.

After the servants quickly changed Jezebel's garments, she and King Ahab led their guests to the banquet hall to the fanfare of trumpets. They walked up to a dais where two goblets of wine for a toast awaited them on their table. The guests took their places and picked up their goblets as well. The two kings, Ethbaal and Ahab, then Eser and Jezebel toasted each other. Queen Jezebel called for success in their great new alliance.

Jezebel was beginning to like Ahab very much. It was not the love created by the life long relationship with Hannibal, or the fiery physical passion she felt for Sikhar. But this was where she needed to be in a relationship. It was one of equals in mind and heart, filled with trust and fulfillment of promises.

This was Jezebel and Aishah becoming truly one with the combined powers of courage and love to move her forward into her new life.

Before dawn the next morning King Ethbaal and Prince Eser started for home. Ethbaal was not feeling well. He thought it might be a hangover from the celebrating. Eser was eager to take him home where his own physician could attend to him.

Jezebel and four of King Ahab's guards mounted horses and rode to the valley below Mount Carmel with them. When they approached the border of Samaria the king was feeling somewhat better. Jezebel was relieved. Reluctantly she bid them farewell and turned back toward Samaria with her guards.

When she went into her rooms at the palace all of the wedding clothing had been removed. Her room furnishings were sparse, but neat, clean, and the room well aired out. The flowers from the celebration were brought in and filled the room with a pleasant fragrance. When a meal was served she asked to have it brought to her rooms.

"Where is King Ahab today?"

"On business, my lady. He left a message for you on your bed."

The servant bowed and left the room. Jezebel went immediately to her bedroom and retrieved the note.

"My dear Queen Jezebel, regrettably I needed to be away today but I will return this evening to have dinner with you. Please forgive me, my dear. I am eager to return home to you. Ahab"

She was pleased at his tender words. This gave her the day to acquaint herself with the rest of the palace. First she would need to order furnishings for her rooms and met with the head servants to give them her plan.

Chapter 38

She went to a far corridor and opened ornate doors at the end. They opened into a huge high-ceiling room with walls of windows. It contained an altar to Baal and beside it was an Asherah to Astarte covered and surrounded by many flowers, jewels and draperies.

Memories of the School of Astarte came flooding back. Jezebel was at home. Tears rolled down her cheeks as she dropped to her knees on a thick floor pad. She praised Astarte and prayed for a long time.

"Are you pleased, my queen?"

She jumped up and turned to see Ahab walking in. He opened his arms and she rushed into them. He held her tightly for a few minutes.

"Yes! I am pleased, even enthralled. It is so beautiful! I am at home with my gods."

"I had it redecorated as a surprise for you. The servants worked for weeks gathering the fabrics and jewels from my treasury and planning every part of it."

"My dear husband, how kind you are! This has touched my heart more deeply than you might imagine."

"I must tell you, Jezebel, there has not been love in my life. I want to know what it is, but I know nothing about it."

"Love? Are you saying you wish there be love between us?"

"I believe so. Are you willing?"

They went to King Ahab's chambers and made love for hours, talking, touching, holding, and consummating their marriage. All of their passion that had been suppressed or channeled in other ways during their lives burst forth and finally they lay exhausted.

She sat up on the side of the bed and pulled a light robe around her shoulders. He smiled up at her, a smile of contentment.

"This is only a small part of love, my husband. You can always depend upon me for comfort. There is much more. It is a promise to treat each other kindly and with great respect whatever is happening around us."

Two servants came into the room, bowed with eyes to the floor, and wordlessly placed their dinner on a table by the bed. Then they stayed bowed and backed out of the room.

"Did I forget to tell you there is no privacy here? The servants pretend to see nothing and know nothing. But they know everything and share it all behind the kitchen hearth with the rest of the servants."

"I assumed as much. I lived in a palace where as a child I naively thought I had secrets. Actually I was watched, laughed at, applauded secretly, and imitated behind my back. My brother eventually told me."

Ahab laughed uproariously.

"I spent time in a storage closet near the back of the hearth so I could listen. Either they did not know I was there, or they knew and were sure my father, Omri, would behead them if they revealed anything."

"Dear husband, how is it you worship Baal and Astarte instead of the Jewish god, Yahweh? I thought Israel was rooted in the Ten Commandments and the anger of this god who punishes the people when they did not obey them."

"My father was the commander of King Elah's army when Zimri assassinated him and took the throne. King Zimri lasted one week and was killed. The troops then chose my father and he took the throne.

"He was not interested in the slave like worship of Yahweh and the constant upbraiding of a prophet called Elijah. So he turned to Baal who blessed but did not punish. Baal was more in line with his aspirations toward conquest of the northern neighbors."

"Does Israel accept your worship of Baal?"

"Yes, Israel does. Judah to the south is another story. They are ready to fight and die for Yahweh, and to kill everyone else. They are fanatics! Called a stiff-necked race. And that they are."

"Who are these prophets? What power do they have in Israel?"

"Let us eat our dinner while I will tell you what I know. I am nearly starving from the business and travel which affords us only a few figs and bread as we keep moving.

"They proclaim Yahweh speaks to them and tells them what the people should do. The prophet Samuel was told by Yahweh to anoint Saul as king, the first king of Israel and so he did. And after that the people also elected Saul.

"I cannot believe Yahweh was very smart because Saul turned out to be a terrible king, disobedient. Samuel was constantly upbraiding him for not waiting for Yahweh's directions through Samuel. Saul was a good warrior, but the prophet drove him insane."

"It all sounds very complicated...hard to know who is in charge. I can understand why your father, you, and all the nations turn to Baal."

"Beware of Elijah, Jezebel. He is loud, relentless, and gathers support of the people by terrorizing them with the wrath of Yahweh. He might do anything when provoked."

That made Jezebel shiver a little.

"What other intrigues might there be I have yet to learn about? Is Ahab's life in danger from this man? Is mine?"

"Take me to see some of our country, Ahab. I want to be with you wherever you need to go."

Did I just say Our country? That sounds so strange to me. I must get Accustomed to thinking of it as our country and...my country. Oh, Phoenicia, how I miss you.

In the morning they left early in a carriage with Ahab's guards. Two horses were tied on the back of the carriage for their use.

"We will go to Jerusalem, the capitol city of Judah, to strengthen the business agreements, and then to Jericho which is hardly a city now. It was built nine thousand years ago and had been destroyed many times.

"I need to meet with Hiel from Bethel to help him with rebuilding the destroyed walls. The walls are needed to secure the population so it can grow and prosper."

"This sounds so familiar to me, Ahab. I have seen the ruined cities of Mesopotamia that also were destroyed over and over."

Jezebel was amazed at Ahab's ability to talk to people and come to agreements that were good for everyone. But there was jeering and rock throwing aimed at them as they passed through the streets of Jerusalem going in and coming out.

Jezebel was a little frightened at the level of hatred and violence against them.

"They call us infidels and sinners. That Yahweh hates Baal and Ahab! These people are vicious! How dare they treat a king this way?"

Jezebel could feel the old angers rising up in her and Aishah was nowhere to be found. She was ready to throw the rocks back and fight them all.

"As you can see these are Elijah's people and he keeps them stirred up with hatred and fear. There is nothing we can do except go about our business, move quickly through the streets, and ignore them."

"Why do they not understand you are trying to do good for them?"

"They only understand we do not worship Yahweh. We worship their Satan, Baal. They understand nothing more."

Chapter 39

A few days later after leaving Jerusalem they started out for Jericho on horseback. The road was steep and rocky as they went down toward the Jordan River. Jezebel did not know much about the terrain they would encounter, but she was told the Dead Sea to the south of Jericho was fourteen hundred feet below the surface of the Great Sea. She kept looking up at the mountains along the Jordan River and imagining that the surface of the Great Sea where the ships were sailing was up there.

She was glad when Jericho was in sight because she was beginning to feel quite nauseated. Ahab saw her turn pale and stopped the horses. The guards helped her down. They spread a blanket under a tree for her to lie down and rest. Ahab sent a guard to Jericho to find Hiel and a physician if there was one.

Hiel and a woman rushed to them.

"We have no physician, but I believe what Queen Jezebel needs is a woman, a midwife, someone who knows women."

It was clear to the midwife Jezebel was with child.

"You should rest in Jericho for a few days, but you are well, my queen. I pray they will make the journey back to Samaria easy for you and not hurry. You must rest along the way."

Ahab was wide-eyed.

"A child? Perhaps a son! This is wonderful!"

"Yes it is my husband. The midwife says I am healthy. It would be good if I were able to rest often on our Journey back to Samaria so I will not lose the child."

They decided to stay a few weeks in Jericho. The midwife attended Jezebel the whole time. Ahab wanted to take the midwife back to Samaria, but Jezebel begged him not to take her from her home.

"Her family and her city needs her, Ahab."

"But you might need her too!"

"The midwife cannot help me along the way. It is up to me to take care of myself. We will get home safely, I am sure. I am strong. I have traveled on camels for months, horses, and ships. The illness I am told is natural for women who are with child and it will not last very long."

"I will help Hiel with his work here. We can start back when you feel it is right. I will be back in a little while for dinner with you."

She smiled at him, not sure food sounded good quite yet. The midwife gave her some powders in wine to settle her stomach and she slept until Ahab returned.

After a week and a few days they started home on horseback until they got up out of the Jordan Valley to a place where the carriage was waiting for them. Jezebel was happy to see the carriage. A guard helped her off the horse and into the carriage. She immediately sat down on the soft cushions of the seat, leaned back, and fell asleep. Ahab climbed in beside her and cradled her in his arms for the rest of the journey.

Eight months later a son was born, Ahaziah, who one day would become the eighth king of the northern Kingdom of Israel. Like his father, Ahab, he would reign from the throne in Samaria.

Eser arrived for a political meeting with Ahab and his officials in time to see the baby. Jezebel was so happy to see Eser. She had missed him so much.

"Ahab went to take documents to the officials in Tirzah after their meeting, so Eser stayed a week with Jezebel. They talked for hours and spent some time riding horses in the countryside. They picnicked on Jezebel's favorite hill where she could see the Great Sea, as Eser had told her.

"Something is on your mind, my brother. I can see it in your eyes."

"Yes, there is. Laila has never fully recovered from the birth of Mattan and is not strong. The midwife and physician have helped her all they can, but it does not look good. She is afraid she will die before Mattan reaches two."

"Oh Eser, I am so sorry. I must go back with you to see her. I promised her I would come back. I will send a message to Ahab so he will know why I am away and bring Ahaziah with me. I cannot bear to leave him with servants while he is so young."

They took a large carriage, her guards, and started for Tyre immediately. Ahaziah was content to be fed and rocked to sleep by the motion of the carriage as it bumped along the roads.

"How is our father doing?"

"He is tired much of the time and has turned many of this duties over to trusted officials. He does not sail anymore and there is a shaking in his hands. He says it is just old age but I think there is something else. Of course he will not discuss it with anyone."

"And what of Shalmaneser? Does he threaten Phoenicia?"

"Not yet. He knows he can take Phoenicia anytime he wants. He is more focused upon Damascus and the King of Aram. There will be a battle between them and then I fear he will set his sights on Israel."

"I am sure Ahab will fight. His army is well trained and he is a good warrior like his father. We will be safe."

Jezebel said that with more conviction than she really felt. The memory of Nimrod and the overwhelming power of its buildings and walls reminded her Shalmaneser would be a strong enemy.

When she saw Laila she was shocked. Laila was pale and thin. She got up off her bed and rushed into Jezebel's arms.

"Oh, my sister, you have come! I feared I would never see you again. As you can see, I am not doing well. I spend most of my days in my bed except to care for Mattan. The servants want to care for him, but I must do it myself as long as I am strong enough."

"Come, Laila, sit down and we can talk. I have someone to show you!"

Eser walked into the room holding tiny Ahaziah. He took the blanket from around his little body and laid him in Laila's arms. Laila burst into tears.

"He is so beautiful! Thank you for bringing him. Is he not young to travel so far?"

"He took the journey quite well. The rocking of the carriage kept him content. He slept most of the way except for when I fed him."

"And your husband, King Ahab? He allowed you to come?"

"It is in my marriage contract I may return home to visit my family. I am sure he did not expect it to be so soon, but neither did I. He was away so I left a message for him. He will wait for me to return or come after me. We will see if the contract is remembered."

"I wish I had your courage, Jezebel. I have always been frail, even as a little child. Eser is so sweet and gentle. I must admit you frightened me when I first met you! You are the first strong woman I ever met."

They laughed and talked together between Laila's naps. While Laila rested Jezebel would go with Eser around Tyre, visiting the trading floor she had seen so long ago and the docks. Oh how she missed the sea and the ships!

Jezebel planned to stay for the week with Eser and Laila. To her surprise King Ethbaal arrived the day after she did. He brought with him all the officials and dignitaries from Sidon for Eser's coronation as King of Tyre.

"I did not know there would be a coronation so soon, but I am happy I am here for it. Were you not going to invite me?"

"I heard you were already here. I sent a message to King Ahab. He should be here shortly. I am concerned about Laila's health and want to hold the ceremony while she is well enough to attend and become Queen Laila. Someday Mattan will need to know his mother was crowned a queen."

"Well, you do have a soft spot in your heart, Father! I will have a servant bring me some appropriate attire for the occasion."

"Good. Good...I must go to speak with Eser."

Jezebel smiled knowing her father would immediately take his leave at any mention of feelings.

Chapter 40

She told Ethbaal about the treatment they received in Jerusalem. "The Jews came out onto the road to throw rocks and dung at us because we do not worship Yahweh. They were so disrespectful to a king! I cannot understand that. I have never seen the people be disrespectful to you, Father. What would you do?"

"I am not sure. Most everyone here worships Baal. If they do not…no one cares. They all go on about their business. The Jews are different. They are fanatical about their god, claim their god led them out of bondage in Egypt thousands of years ago, through the desert, and into Canaan. Then this god gave them all of Canaan. They call it the Promised Land. So they fight to the death for everything for their god."

"Why can they not just keep to their religion, worship their god, and let everyone else worship theirs? Why do they care what I or anyone else does?"

"They have prophets who declare their god speaks to them. Yahweh commands them to kill all infidels or drive them out and secure their Holy Land. They fight oppressors for a god that seems to oppress them.

"People of other nations can be hard to understand. Be careful, Jezebel. Keep your guards close by. You and Ahab will always be the focus of their hatred."

A whirl of activity hummed in every area of the palace. King Ethbaal spoke privately with Eser and his reason for having the ceremony and crowning now.

"Not only is Laila frail, but I am not doing so well myself. I need you to be the king before something happens to me or Laila. I pray Laila gets her strength soon. I brought everything we need including attire, crowns, and the financial support to get everything put in proper order."

It was amazing how well it all came together. King Ahab arrived with his retinue and gifts for the new king. The coronation was beautiful and Laila was beaming. Jezebel stayed close to her should the ceremony be too long and tax her strength. They were both proud of Eser as he stood straight and tall, receiving the crown, scepter, and mantle of the throne with manly grace.

The banquet went late into the night. Laila retired very early. Jezebel looked in on her from time to time. Eser broke away from the festivities to look in on her as well.

Ahab was eager to speak with Jezebel and to see his son. They met in a private beautifully decorated palace room. Jezebel put her arms around Ahab and leaned into his chest until little sleeping Ahaziah was brought in by a serving girl. They held him and cooed to him until he began to fuss and the serving girl quickly swept him away to be changed.

"It seems our messages were not timed well, my husband. I had no idea all of this was happening. My concern was for Laila. I hope my leaving did not cause you distress."

"I was in Tirzah and the messages were late both ways. But now we are here together at another great celebration. It seems our son has grown in the last few weeks!"

"Yes, he has. And I have missed you."

Jezebel pulled Ahab down on a chaise, opened her robe, and wrapped her legs around him. He covered them both with his robe and they made love. Jezebel felt such peace and contentment in the warmth of his body next to hers. Any tension between them melted away.

With King Baal Eser II now on the throne and Queen Laila recovering from the festivities, Jezebel, Ahab, and Ahaziah began the journey home. Baby Ahaziah slept in his father's arms for most of the way. Ahab was pleased and smiled at both of them.

There was bad news when they returned. Hiel's sons had been killed in

Jericho while they were building the walls and setting up the gates. Some stones high up on the wall fell on them knocking down part of the gates. They were both crushed.

"How awful! Ahab, you must go to Hiel now. He needs you!"

Ahab and a unit of guards rode for Jericho the next morning. When they arrived, Hiel's men were still trying to get the bodies of his sons out from under the huge wall stones. Ahab's guards rushed to help. Ahab found Hiel sitting under a tree sobbing and inconsolable.

"It is the curse of Joshua! He said anyone who tried to rebuild Jericho would pay with his sons' lives. I should have sent them away!"

Women from Jericho brought burial cloths. When the bodies were finally recovered the women wrapped them before Hiel saw them.

"Should I not see them?"

"My dear friend, remember them as they were. It is enough to know they are now dead. There is no need to see them crushed. Where shall we bury them?"

"Place one under the wall and one under the gates as was the prophecy, that I may bless them each time I see the wall and gates."

The workers did as Hiel requested. They set special stones around them to protect them so long as Jericho stood.

In Samaria, Jezebel realized she was again with child. The morning sickness was mercifully short this time. The midwives' potions relieved it quickly.

Worse than morning sickness was a man in the hills near the palace who was shouting at Ahab, accusing him of sinning against the Lord. He kept it up for days until Jezebel sent the guards to chase him away.

"Ahab, who is this man shouting from the hills and who is this lord he says you are sinning against?"

"He is a popular prophet who travels Israel and Judah proclaiming Yahweh as the only god and anyone who disobeys Yahweh is sinning and doomed. He proclaims worship of Baal and Astarte is evil and we are evil doers. It is said he performs miracles in the name of Yahweh. The people believe him and spread his lies."

"I had our guards chase him away after a few days of his shouting.

But why do you not chase him out of Samaria back to Judah? Have him imprisoned, even executed?"

"We do chase him away but of course he always comes back more vehement than ever. He hides in caves in the hills and my guards have more important things to do than chase the old pest. To kill him would cause an uprising in Judah.

"My father worked to unite Judah and Israel. His murder would separate us and cause a civil war again. I have enough to do watching for the aggressions of Shalmaneser in Nimrod and Ben-hadad who is rising in Damascus."

"No one should be allowed to harass the king and queen or any royalty."

"True, my wife, but one must pick ones battles carefully. Some are not worth fighting. They take the energy away from the bigger, more threatening ones. You might remember what I have said when challenges come your way, which they surely will."

"I do remember all you tell me. You may recall I pledged to defend you from your enemies. They may be smaller ones, but enemies none the less. Rather than attacking the whole country, they eat away at its foundations. You may be assured I will do my best not to let that happen."

Chapter 41

He led her to his chambers and slipped her robe from her shoulders. "Be gentle, my love. I am with child again."

"Am I not always gentle?"

"There are times when you are not. I enjoy that, too…but there is a child to consider."

"Another son and so soon?"

"Perhaps…"

He picked her up and laid her on his bed, his robe covering them both.

Jezebel spent her days managing Ahab's tasks while he was away. Occasionally she sent trumpeters to the walls to blow loud horns to drown out Elijah's shouts when he got especially annoying. That would quiet him for a while.

King Ben-hadad of Aram was a constant challenge for Ahab, causing skirmishes along the border. He gathered thirty-two kings and marched against Samaria. Then he sent messengers to Ahab demanding Ahab's complete surrender.

Ahab called the elders and the people of Israel into council. They refuted the demands of Ben-hadad. Ben-hadad then threatened to make dust of Samaria.

Ahab mustered seven thousand men and marched. He sent a messenger to a very drunk Ben-hadad warning him not to brag while putting his armor on, but while taking it off! The Israelites killed one hundred thousand Aramean foot-soldiers in one day. The rest fled to Aphek.

Ben-hadad and his guards crawled to Ahab's chariot to beg for their lives. A treaty was made between them that Ben-hadad would restore all the towns and the bazaars in Damascus taken from King Omri, Ahab's father. Ahab let him live.

"What? You let him live after he attacked Samaria? That is unheard of! Ahab, why?"

"Jezebel, remember when I said to pick your battles carefully? A greater war is coming with Shalmaneser. We will need every man we can muster in the war against him. Ben-hadad is beholden to me for his life now. He will not shame himself again by attacking Samaria."

Jezebel worried about the prophets now on Ahab's payroll, whom all the kings depended upon for advice about coming battles.

"Why do you listen to these prophets who are not Baal's priests? They worship Yahweh. They hate us! They predict victory so you will keep paying them. Someday they will cause a disaster for Israel!"

"It is just tradition, my queen, and it keeps Elijah quiet. I do not listen to their prattle. I make my own decisions about battles."

Jezebel was determined to be true to her promise. She would protect Ahab from his enemies. She paid whisperers to start a rumor that "a lying spirit" was among the prophets. She knew it was one of their most feared superstitions. They would soon be at each other's throats.

King Eser arrived in Samaria without advanced notice. Jezebel ran into his arms and kissed his cheek.

"What is it, my brother? What brings you here unannounced?"

"Is Ahab here?"

"No, he is away. He would be here had he known you were coming. What has happened? Tell me!"

"Our father has died. He has been ill and weak. He died in his sleep."

"Oh, no!"

Jezebel collapsed into his arms and wept on his shoulder.

They walked into Jezebel's private rooms and sat down. She ordered her personal serving woman to bring food and wine.

"We have lost a dear friend, my brother. He was our bulwark against the world. Our protector."

"Now it is just us. We must be a friend to our families and make them feel safe."

"And Laila? How is she?"

"Doing quite well. Her servants love her and take good care of her and Mattan."

"I keep wishing I were in Tyre with you instead of Samaria. There are enemies everywhere here. Ahab does not see them, but I do."

"He is accustomed to larger enemies and so was his father. He is a warrior."

She sucked in a deep breath and reached for the wine, handing one to Eser.

"And so am I! It is time I remembered that. Being afraid will not help."

"You sound more like my sister! How is little Ahaziah?"

"Crawling everywhere, pulling things down onto his head and the floor. He keeps his servants running after him. But he is about to have some competition for their attention. I am with child again."

"What? How soon?"

"Many months yet. I just recovered from the pesky morning sickness. That did not help my moods. I sound as if I gave gotten whiney!"

"I wish I could take you back to Tyre with me, but I have an errand in Damascus now that Ahab has won the victory. There are cities and market places to be turned over to Samaria and treaties to be signed."

"How long can you stay with me?"

"A few days. When will Ahab return?"

"I do not know. I just know when he gets here. There are many of his duties I have taken over. He is beginning to depend upon me to see to everything here. That is good because I can keep others from taking advantage of him."

"Who would do that?"

"The prophets he pays. It is tradition for kings to have prophets who predict their victories, but I know they are a danger. They are liars and thieves. I have faithful spies who report on them to me."

"I see...I will stay for a week. I want to see these prophets."

Eser went to the gathering place of the prophets.

"Who are you, son of Baal? Why are you here?"

"I am indeed a son of Baal, here to learn why you prophets of Yahweh lie to your king. One of your commandments from your god is you shall not bear false witness. In other words you shall not lie!"

"We do not lie! The king pays us to tell him what he wishes to hear."

"Then you are not prophets! You are paid liars!"

When they picked up stones to throw at him, Eser's guards came forward with weapons drawn and the prophets scurried back to their tents.

"Great Astarte, Eser, they would have killed you!"

"I am sure that is true."

He repeated the conversation to her.

"Now we have proof from their own lips what you have suspected. Will Ahab believe you?"

"Ahab will not even listen. He thinks they are nothing. His mind is on coming wars."

Chapter 42

Weeks later Ahab came storming into the palace and sat down to drink and sulk. He would not eat or talk.

"Who are you? Where is my husband, Ahab! You are surely not he!"

He ignored her and turned away. Jezebel became angry.

"Ahab! Speak to me! What has disturbed you? I have much to tell you and we must work together."

"One of the prophets disguised himself and ran alongside my horse shouting since I let Ben-hadad go my life would be taken according his lord. And my people taken for his people."

"Ahab, let me tell you what I must. Eser was here and confronted these so called prophets you pay. They admitted to him they are liars and thieves. You were victorious! Why do you let them bother you?"

"Eser was here? Where is he now?"

"He came to tell me our father, King Ethbaal, died. Now he has gone to Damascus to get your treaties signed and be sure they are honored by Ben-hadad."

Ahab gave a sigh and set his drink aside.

"I am aggrieved to hear King Ethbaal has died. He was a good friend. Sometimes I think he was my only real friend."

"I am your friend, Ahab. I always will be."

"It seems you and Eser have more faith in me than I have in myself lately."

"What is making you lose your faith? Surely not these false prophets! As you have said, they are nothing."

"And I am almost nothing according to the prophets. Maybe it is true."

He struggled to his feet. He could hardly stand so she helped him to his chamber. He flopped down on the bed and began snoring. She sat beside him until a servant came in with a potion for his stomach and hangover. Ahab awakened momentarily, drank the potion Jezebel offered, and fell back on the bed asleep.

Jezebel left his rooms and returned to hers. She pulled out a bundle from the corner of the room and began carefully sifting through it. The servants had not unpacked it because she ordered them not to. At the bottom was her precious stack of goat skins, the memoirs she had begun when traveling with the caravan. Sitting down at a table and sorting them to find the last page, she began to write.

Caravans come and go. Empires rise and fall. Others arise in their place. Is this how it happens? Their king gives up, hiding in drink and giving into human weakness. Will he be forgiven a defeat as he did Ben-hadad? If not, can I save the kingdom without him? Or should I go home to Phoenicia? But what would I do there? It belongs to Eser. No, I must stay for my sons to rule this kingdom when I am gone. This is my destiny.

Joram was born to Jezebel and Ahab. He would become the ninth king of the northern kingdom of Israel. Her labor was easy and the baby was healthy. Ahab was away fighting border skirmishes with Syria and quelling the Moabite uprising.

Ahaziah was thrilled to have a little brother. His life had been lonely at the palace except for the servants who would bring their children to play with him from time to time.

Jezebel sent a message to Ahab that the child was born but there was no response. She was not sure if he were wounded, dead, or did not care.

She held court every day, receiving messengers, diplomats, and settling disputes. Her personal scribe kept meticulous accounts of all the decisions and transactions. Messengers from Eser were especially welcome. They were given precedence while the others were instructed to wait.

Someone was always unhappy with her decisions. They clamored for

Ahab to return to these duties. Of course he did not. He was away for longer and longer periods of time leaving everything to her.

Jezebel spent some time every day in the beautiful temple of Baal and Astarte that Ahab gave her as a wedding gift. It calmed her to call upon Aishah and remember all she was taught at the School of Astarte. Closing her eyes the peaceful memories of that time to flood back into her mind. She could see Ashara coming to greet her and enfolding her in love.

Her reverie was occasionally interrupted when Ahaziah would break loose from Jezebel's servant and dash into the temple to climb on her lap. She cuddled him and kissed him. Then he would run back to the servant and resume their play in Joram's nursery. He was growing so fast. She was amazed at how the years were slipping by.

Elijah returned to the hills of Samaria to shout his accusations at Jezebel. When Ahab returned Elijah's threats became louder. They were shouted at him as well. Over Jezebel's objections Ahab would go out into the hills to find Elijah and promise to worship Yahweh.

"How can you give in to him? You make yourself look foolish. Baal is your god and your father, Omri's, god! Do you want priests of Baal to shout at you, too, so you will remember that?"

"Elijah confuses me! Why can I not worship all of them? I even placed Yahweh's altars next to Astarte's Asherahs. Why does anyone care who I worship?"

"Ahab, you are not confused! You are allowing him to weaken you. You must not let him for your children's sake if not mine!"

Ahab jumped up suddenly filled with rage.

"So you think I am weak, my queen? Let me prove to you I am still strong! Come with me!"

He pulled her into his bed chamber, tore off her tunic and pushed her onto the bed.

"Ahab, stop this!"

"Stop? And be thought weak? I will not!"

After raping Jezebel, Ahab stormed out of the palace without stopping to see his children. It was clear he was expressing his fear in violence and she was relieved when he left. She did not know if he had ever seen Joram. He most likely went back to his troops and more battle plans.

She so wanted to go back to Tyre to see Eser, but he might not be there. It was obvious she had no escape now. She was held here by her children and what was now her country. She was Queen Jezebel of Israel and she must face whatever the future would bring and not run away.

She resolved not to speak with Ahab about Elijah or anything else he might be doing. She would not ask about battles and only respond when he asked questions.

There would be no more forcible sex or other violence against her. She knew what to do.

Chapter 43

The winds of war were blowing more fiercely toward Israel now. There were meetings of kings and generals in Samaria, Tirzah, and Damascus. The iron workers were furiously turning out weapons and young men were eager to join the ranks of the military. Jezebel remembered Shalmaneser's graciousness on their visit and it was hard to envision that he was now out to destroy them.

The war years dragged on and on. People came to her court every day in fear asking to know what would happen to them. It was Jezebel's opportunity to stand strong and strengthen the people.

"King Ahab and all the twelve other kings with him are amassing troops to keep us safe. Your young men are strong and dedicated. I promise you Israel will stand and nothing will defeat her. Be strong for your communities and families. Let no one be afraid!"

Some of them went away encouraged and some doubtful. But Jezebel did not waver. She always continued tell them to do the same. In the face of all that was before her, children, duties, wars, and the change in Ahab, she found it more difficult to find time to spend in Baal's temple in the palace to feel Aishah's heart in her.

Her personal scribe had a son who wished to be a scribe as well. Jezebel decided it would be perfect to engage him in writing her memoirs. His name was Joshua. He was adorably shy with black curly hair. He came to her promptly with leaves of papyrus, a bush and ink pot, ready to begin.

"Joshua, did you make the ink brush yourself? I have not seen one like it."

"Yes, Your Highness. It is easier to hold and makes clearer strokes. My father now uses one like it. I made it for him."

"That is wonderful! We will work for short periods of time. I may say things that make you uncomfortable. You do understand Ahab and I worship Baal and Astarte?"

"Yes, Your Highness. Whatever you say is all right with me. I will work as long as you need me to."

Jezebel drew a deep breath, smiled at him, and gathered her thoughts.

"Thank you, Joshua. Let us begin."

He dipped his brush into the ink and waited.

I am Queen Jezebel, daughter of King Ethbaal of Sidon and Tyre. I am the High Priestess in the Phoenician religion of Baal and Astarte, god and goddess, who have attended my every waking moment with power and riches. I am the priestess of their temples, guardian of their altars and sacred places. I intend to maintain the alliance between Israel and Phoenicia...

She stopped and looked to see if Joshua was keeping up.

"Oh yes, Your Highness! I am easily writing every word and miss none of them."

"That is very good, Joshua. Let us continue."

I never knew my birth mother, but it did not matter. Astarte was my mother and my servants tended to every need...

She talked on for a long period of time.

My father knew Ahab needed our alliance and we needed him for protection. He must have convinced Ahab I would be a good queen...

Jezebel stopped again for a moment to gather her thoughts. Joshua looked up and smiled with brush poised over the papyrus.

My brother, Baal Eser II, carried a list of conditions that must be met for me to agree to this marriage...

It is the custom as a foreign wife of a king I be allowed to continue my own religion in Israel...

It had been another hour. She stopped and watched him finish his writing.

"Did you get all of that, Joshua?"

"Yes, Your Highness."

"This will be all for today. You are to show these memoirs to no one. Do you understand?"

"May I show them to my father, your senior scribe, for any corrections in the spelling that might be needed?"

"Yes, you may. Be sure the words remain exactly as I have said them."

Joshua bowed, tucked the papyrus under his arm, gathered his brush and ink pot, and left.

Jezebel knew the physical symptoms. She was again with child. Ahab had a habit of returning for a day and leaving again without seeking her out. For the next four years he came and went without telling her.

"Ahab, may I have a moment to speak with you?"

"Why? Is not the business of ruling going well for you?"

"The business of rule goes well. You have another child, a daughter was born. She is four years old. I wish this to be the last one. You have two male heirs to the throne."

"I understand you perfectly. And I do not wish to cause you to have more children."

"Ahab, what happened to love? Are we not still to be husband and wife?"

"When I forgave Ben-hadad, you called me weak. My father called me weak. He said I was soft. Perhaps he was right. Love makes a man weak."

Jezebel was saddened at this and tears threatened to come. She turned and walked back into her private rooms to be alone and think.

Would Seti or Sikhar have turned on me like this? Perhaps not, but Seti was without position and Sikhar was a stable owner. My destiny was not with them and that I am sure. But what about Aishah? Is she not part of my destiny, too? Does destiny trample love? Must it be so cruel?

For twelve years the war went on, battles, defeats, starvation, and wreckage everywhere. War was almost at their borders many times. Ahab and Ben-hadad led twelve kings and over one hundred thousand men, chariots, horses, and camels north toward Qarqar to drive Shalmaneser back.

Though the battles were long and vicious, Ahab and Ben-hadad and their allies were victorious. After that there were six more battles still to be won.

Chapter 44

When Athaliah was born, she was red-faced, crying and kicking, and waving her little fists. She would not be comforted. The midwife shook her head as she wrapped her in swaddling clothes.

"This one will be a handful, Your Highness. She will challenge you for your throne!"

"Her name is Athaliah and yes I believe you are right. She has already begun to fight against the world into which she is born! She will demand a place of her choosing."

Athaliah continued her combative behaviors as she grew up. Her dark hair was wild and she carried weapons to threaten her brothers. Jezebel was disappointed. She and her daughter would not be friends. But then Athaliah was the product of a violent rape. That might explain it.

Ahab came home, war weary and needing rest. He stayed in his private quarters and drank for days. Remembering earlier times when she hoped he might love her, Jezebel looked in on him from time to time.

He was snoring loudly. She did not make her presence known.

It was clear she no longer knew this man.

Elijah continued his rampage and harassment. He shouted continually for Ahab to come to him. Ahab went out to meet Elijah, leaning heavily on a walking stick to steady himself. He was lame from battle and woozy from drinking. Jezebel watched in disgust from the palace wall.

Ahab shouted back at him.

"You are a troubler of Israel! Go away!"

"You and Jezebel have sinned against Yahweh and there will be a drought in the land."

"Elijah! Why do you keep punishing Israel, bringing destruction? You bring threats and drought upon the people who have done nothing to you, nor have they sinned!"

"I have not brought the drought! You have done it because of your sin! Renounce Baal worship and turn to Yahweh before it is too late. You and Jezebel will die and the dogs will eat your blood!"

"I know nothing of Yahweh! I and my father before me have always worshipped Baal. Baal does not threaten me but gives me victory after victory! Jezebel is a priestess of Astarte since she was born. We do not prevent the people from worshipping Yahweh, Baal, or the Canaanite gods. Solomon's one hundred foreign wives brought their own gods.

"And you Elijah! You have not succeeded in turning Israel to Yahweh! You have failed! Failed your god! And now you shout at me! You are weak, old man. Go away!"

Elijah stomped away pounding his walking stick on the stones and hard ground. He sought out his cave in the hills beyond the palace. Furious, Ahab followed after him.

An incensed Jezebel watched the whole scene. She knew Ahab's drunken bluster would not stand up long. He would crumble in the face of Elijah's demands. It was time for her to go after Elijah again.

Ahab came back to the palace after two days, ragged and distraught.

"Have you promised him we will now worship Yahweh, my husband? Are you now worshipping Elijah's god?"

"You see the drought! Would it hurt to do that in case it is true?"

"I am not frightened by Elijah's lies. For every Asherah he destroys I put back two in its place. Do something to show Yahweh's priests to be frauds! We must prove Baal is more powerful!"

"And just how will you do that, my queen?"

"I will shame or kill them all in your name, my king!"

Ahab stomped off to his chambers to change his clothes. He came out again and ordered his horses and chariot to be brought around. He could hardly climb into it because of his injuries from the wars. He grasped the rail, pulled himself up, and took the reins. He set the team galloping away toward Tirzah, Omri's old capitol, to clear his mind.

Jezebel gathered her four hundred and fifty priests of Baal into the great hall of the palace and laid out her plan.

"Elijah is challenging us with the ridiculous claim his god is more powerful than Baal and Astarte, who have blessed us forever. Elijah's priests of Yahweh will try to trick you. They plan to kill all of you. You must be ready! Set upon them at the first sign of treachery. In the name of Baal and Astarte, you must not let them defeat you!"

The priests of Baal nodded. They talked and agreed among themselves, and bowed to Jezebel as they departed. Elijah brought his one hundred priests to call out the priests of Baal. His test was to carve a bull and place half of it on each altar with no fire. The priests were to start the fire on the altars by calling to their god to rain down fire from above.

All the priests met on Mount Carmel for the contest. There was much pageantry and louder taunts. Crowds of people came from everywhere to Mount Carmel to witness the contest. The priests of Baal did their rituals, but lightning struck Elijah's altar instead of theirs and set it afire. Then the priests of Yahweh and the crowd of people set upon the priests of Baal with weapons and slaughtered them all.

Jezebel was shocked and livid. To add to her vengeful state of mind, the drought was ending about that time. Elijah declared he, Elijah himself, had opened the heavens and allowed the rain to fall.

"Do you see my power and the power of Yahweh, Jezebel? I alone open and close the heavens. I will see to your demise and all of Baal with you!"

"I am coming for you, Elijah! I will do worse to you than you did to my priests. You will not survive this day!"

She set out in a chariot driving her horses at full gallop.

Elijah was terrified and ran for his life toward the hills like a frightened deer.

Ahab found no respite in Tirzah. There were no battles at the moment and his armies had gone home to their families. He came home weary and feeling lost. He wandered into the city. In an attempt to reassert his power, he offered to buy Naboth's vineyards for an exorbitant price.

"But my lord, I cannot sell the vineyards! They have been in my family for generations. Your offer is most generous, but my family and all those before me who have gone to sleep with the fathers would never forgive me!"

Ahab raised the offer adding two larger vineyards, but Naboth would not agree to sell. Ahab went home feeling utterly defeated and stayed drunk in his chambers for a week.

Chapter 45

Jezebel called Joshua to come and continue writing her memoirs. Joshua came immediately, eager to get started. He was a little hesitant as he sensed Jezebel's anger.

"Have I displeased you, Your Highness?"

"No, Joshua, you please me very much. Let us begin."

The Hebrew people hate me and run away at the sight of my priests and pageants...

As my father promised, I am in truth the king. Ahab has begun to fail now at everything...

I have begged Ahab to stop his constant drinking and return to the throne, but he will not listen...

She had spoken for over an hour and became emotionally exhausted.

"Are you tired, Joshua? Would you like to stop now?"

"I can continue for a little longer if that would please Your Highness."

"I am tired and prefer to stop. I will call you when I am ready to continue."

Months went by. The winter rains had not come and the winds were ferocious, covering everything with sand. Still Elijah shouted at Jezebel from the hillsides.

"Your evil has brought this blight upon the people! Yahweh will punish you and the world will forget you!"

Despite the dust storms, she went out in her chariot to see that her altars were undamaged. The horses reared and stamped at the blustering winds and stinging sand, but she drove them on.

The altars were undisturbed and deserted. The people were hovering close to their homes. It was a relief to return to the protection of the palace walls and out of the wind. The servants kept busy sweeping out the dirt and sand, and shaking out the tapestries and carpets.

Standing at a window Jezebel's thoughts assailed her. *"A drought lingers in the land and Samaria is as dust. I should have hunted and killed Elijah before now. It is Elijah who brings evil upon the people. The day will come when the wind ceases and I will finish this! Ahab listens to Elijah and trembles like a cur at his every word. But I am not afraid of him. I will bring an end to this if it is the last thing I do!"*

She went often to her bath and the oils to relieve her skin of the damage by the stinging sand and wind. It was the only place where she could relax and be at peace for a while.

Jezebel's patience was wearing thin. She was determined to shock Ahab out of his stupor.

"The priests of Yahweh tricked our priests of Baal and slaughtered every one of them! Do you not care? What could possibly be so bad that you drink yourself half to death? What is it you really want, Ahab?"

"I offered to buy Naboth's vineyard for a very good price and he refused me!"

His lips were pursed in a pout and his eyes were red rimmed from the wine. He leaned back on his cushion holding a bunch of grapes with a shaking hand.

"I want to plant a garden next to the palace walls where it will be protected, but Naboth's vineyards are there. So I must purchase his lands for my garden, but he refuses to sell them to me."

"You want to plant a garden? Why do we need a garden? What do you plan to do if he will not sell?"

"I want a garden and that is enough! I do not want to alienate him, so I thought someone else could approach him for me. Not saying it is I behind the offer of course."

"And if he still will not sell?"

"I do not know. I do not understand the man. My offer is more than generous."

"What was his reason for refusing?"

"It belonged to his family for generations. He cannot sell what belongs to all of them."

Jezebel gave a sigh of resignation. *"A vineyard? Why does he need a vineyard? Is he losing his mind?"*

"I will take care of the matter, my husband."

He grumbled something and left. He cloaked himself against the blasting winds and went into the hills to be away from all that reminded him of his impotence.

Jezebel wrote letters to the highest officials using Ahab's seal, as she always did. She proclaimed a feast in his name. She would plant whisperers among the guests that Naboth had blasphemed against their god. She knew their fears and they would drive Naboth to sell to Ahab and leave Samaria.

The feast did not go as Jezebel planned. Instead of convincing Naboth to sell his vineyards and driving him away, they chased him to the outer walls of the city and stoned him to death along with several of their own officials.

It made Jezebel nearly sick to her stomach. She stayed in her chambers for two days. She went to the altars of Baal and Astarte in the palace and tried to pray. She tried to reach within herself to Aishah and remember Ashtara, but it was useless. It was becoming hard to believe that part of her life had even happened.

She was jolted out of her thought by Ahaziah and Joram running hollering through the palace halls, Athaliah behind them with a large club and sword. She was shouting and laughing.

"Naboth is dead and the vineyards are ours! Yay, Naboth is dead!"

Jezebel went out and grabbed her by the hair and pulled her down onto the floor.

"What do you think you are doing? Stop right now. Where did you hear that?"

"I heard it from the servants! I am so proud of you and father! Naboth is dead and…"

Jezebel slapped her hard.

"I said stop right now and do not ever say that again, do you hear me?"

Athaliah jerked herself up from the floor and burst into tears.

"When will you be proud of me? You hate me! I am just like you. Do you hate yourself, too?"

"Athaliah…no, I do not hate you. You are not just like me…I will be proud of you when you begin to act like a princess instead of a warrior. Leave your brothers alone and tend to your studies!"

Chapter 46

Jezebel wondered if she should send Athaliah to Byblos, but she could not let Ashara see what had become of her and her daughter. Had she come to hate herself? No. But hate her life and what it caused her to become, yes. But she would never tell Athaliah that.

Ahaziah was maturing fast. He sat with Jezebel every day as she held court and made decisions. He became her advisor and sounding board. He was so like Eser, picking up quickly on everything. He, too, kept the details of transactions in his records and in his mind. He even looked a little like Eser. It would being tears threatening to roll down her cheeks.

Word came from Eser that Laila had died. Jezebel immediately ordered a carriage to go to Tyre. She called Ahaziah to come with her and ordered Athaliah to stay in Samaria.

"I will not stay behind! I am coming too!"

"No, you may not! Aunt Laila has died and I cannot trust you to behave like royalty."

Athaliah ran to get a horse from the stable to follow them. Jezebel's guards caught up with her and took her back to the palace. She fought them all the way but they were accustomed to handling her tantrums.

Joram was happy to go to the military camp where he spent most of his time. He loved the military and he could escape Athaliah's rages there.

Eser was so happy to see Jezebel and Ahaziah. It had been a long time even though they did their best to be in touch with each other. Jezebel hopped out of the carriage and ran into his arms.

"I am so sorry, Eser. She was a dear sister and I loved her."

"We always knew it was coming, and she did live to see Mattan grow up which is what she hoped for. Ahaziah, you have grown up too!"

They reached out and clapped each other's shoulders. Mattan came out of the palace and shouted to Ahaziah.

"Cousin! Welcome! Come with me and let us talk. There is much catching up to do. Tell me all about Samaria."

The two went off into the palace gardens leaving Jezebel and Eser to go into the palace chapel. The casket and tomb were readied to receive Queen Laila's body. Mattan and Ahaziah came in later for the ceremony and they all mourned Laila's passing together.

"Eser, why does destiny have to be such a hard task master? Now you are alone and Ahab has all but abandoned me. He stays drunk at the palace until he goes off to a battle somewhere."

"We have each other and our children. Even though we are far away. There is not a day goes by I do not think of you. Laila spoke of you often. She loved you. It gave me much joy that you loved her, too."

"Oh, Eser, I have made some terrible mistakes. Hundreds of Elijah's people murdered all four hundred fifty of Baal's priests trying to prove Yahweh was more powerful than Baal. It was like war! I should never have sent them to meet Elijah's priests. I did not know hundreds of Elijah's people would come there, too, and attack them with weapons."

They talked on over dinner and Jezebel was gathering the courage to tell him about Naboth.

"Great Astarte, Eser, I sent whisperers to start a rumor. I thought they would encourage him to sell or chase him from the country, but they chased him and their own officials outside of the city walls and stoned them all to death!"

Jezebel broke down in tears and reached for her wine.

"I am sorry, my brother. It has all been such a disappointment. Even my daughter, who I refused to bring, is a harridan! You thought I was bad when we were kids…well, Athaliah is many times worse than I was, and she is not yet grown."

"And Joram?"

"He is still young and enjoys being among the soldiers. He stays in their military training camps and practices their battle exercises. He hopes Ahab will pay attention to him and be proud, but Ahab does not. I do not think Ahab remembers he has a second son.

"I no longer have high hopes for the future. I just go along day by day as life requires me to do."

"But then there is Ahaziah! What a wonderful young man! You must be proud of him, are you not?"

"Oh, yes! He is so much like you. He was born loving peace and negotiation. But there is a mean world waiting for him in Israel. If he is crowned king in the midst of all this strife, I do not know what will become of him."

"Would you leave him here with me for a few months? Then I promise I will return him."

Jezebel laughed and agreed to let Ahaziah stay, although the palace in Samaria would be empty without him. She saw him as her only ally there.

Mattan and Ahaziah were thrilled. They made plans to visit the Trading Center and the docks. They would sail to Sidon and maybe Byblos to meet the Egyptian ships that traded there. Ahaziah wanted to know all about Phoenicia first hand.

Jezebel stayed with Eser for another week until Mattan and Ahaziah started off on their adventures. It brought memories of her journeys with Eser to those very places and beyond.

Chapter 47

As Jezebel got into her carriage she turned to Eser.

"You will not send them on a camel caravan, will you?"

"No, dear sister. Assyria is much too dangerous now. We were fortunate to visit there when it was peaceful. I think father had a premonition of the future wars and sent us at the right time. I will send him home with a guard and perhaps I can come with him. I love you."

"I love you too, my dear brother."

Ahab was having a loud argument with Elijah when Jezebel came back. She could always hear their shouts ringing through the hills.

"Ahab! Ahab, how could you do this to Naboth? He was a good man. He took care of the poor and widows. The vineyard made it possible for him to do that. It belonged to his father, and his father's father before him. How could you take his vineyard from him?"

"Well, I did not exactly take it from him, Elijah. I offered him a good price, two vineyards of twice the size! He had no reason to deny me. I am the king! I made him a good and fair offer."

"And what of the riot at the festival you proclaimed? Who were the whisperers, the liars you and Jezebel hired? Naboth and several others are dead! Murdered, Ahab, by your queen and with your permission! You knew what she would do."

Ahab shouted in panic.

"It was Jezebel! I knew nothing about the festival or what went on. She said she would get the vineyard for me, but I did not know how she planned to do it! I swear an oath I did not! I never asked her or anyone to kill Naboth."

Elijah shook his head.

"Ahab, you know Jezebel's ways! She will murder to get what she wants! You cannot claim innocence."

"And can you claim innocence for murdering all my priests of Baal? You murder to get what you want, too!"

"I do Yahweh's work! Getting rid of Baal worship in our land is Yahweh's work."

"So, Yahweh is a murderer too, Elijah! You cannot sin and hide behind your god. Your commandment says you shall not kill!"

Elijah ran off into the hills and Ahab came storming into the palace.

"Ahab..."

"Leave me alone, Jezebel."

"Queen Laila has died..."

He shook his head and went into his chambers for some wine.

Jezebel continued holding court and used Ahaziah's records as a guide. It was good to review the decisions and her reasoning. His financial records were a clear picture of all the palace expenses, supplies, servants, guards and repairs. She felt a little more settled as she launched into the business aspect. Everything seemed to be under control for now.

Ahaziah returned to Samaria full of tales of his adventures with Mattan. They were not always on their own. Eser went with them to some places to keep them from trouble he knew lurked there. Assyrians were still occupying some ports in the north. Jezebel listened with fascination and nostalgia to what used to be life for her and Eser.

Ahab came in and announced he was leaving for Jerusalem to arrange a marriage for Athaliah to Prince Jehoram who would become the king of Judah. Jezebel was stunned.

"You are going to betroth her into that murdering family? Jehoram is a monster! She is too young. Can you not wait and find a more suitable marriage for her?"

"It is a suitable marriage! I need to keep Judah under my control."

"Keeping all of Judah under your control will be far easier than keeping Athaliah under your control. You have never bothered to know your daughter. Perhaps she will give you and Judah what you all deserve."

He stood and stared at her stupefied.

"Are you what I deserved, my dear wife?"

"Yes, I am. I have raised your family, kept Israel together, defended you from your enemies, held court every day and taken care of the finances of this palace while you are away. You have tended to none of these things.

"I believe I deserved better from you, Ahab. I have always done my best for you and you have turned away from me, from our bed, and from friendship. Perhaps expecting love was too much. But I have done nothing to deserve your hatred and drunken outbursts."

Tears were hot behind her eyes. Ahab turned and stomped away.

"I am going to Jerusalem."

"He is going to do what, Mother? Marry that slime? He cannot do that! I will kill them all!"

Jezebel smiled and put an arm around Athaliah's shoulders, something she had not done for several years.

"I am sure you will, my daughter. I am sure you will."

Ahab began to eye Ramoth-Gilead, a city which belonged to Israel, but was in the possession of Syria. As always Ahab avoided saying anything directly to the king of Syria to keep on his good side. Instead, Ahab became downcast and moody. Then he began to quarrel with the king of Syria over other things and the alliance was broken.

That was the end of three years of peace between Syria and Israel. Ahab went to King Jehoshaphat of Judah for help.

"Do you know Ramoth-Gilead belongs to us? Yet we are doing nothing to take it out of the hand of the King of Aram? Will you go with me to battle for our city, Ramoth-Gilead?"

Chapter 48

Jehoshaphat agreed on the condition they would consult the prophets first.

Reluctantly Ahab gathered four-hundred prophets together. There was mass confusion and hysteria!

At the gate of Samaria, sitting on their respective thrones, were the king of Israel and the king of Judah arrayed in their most glorious robes, surrounded by all the prophets prophesying in loud voices. Each one shouted louder than the next, vying for the attention of the invisible god.

After hours of this cacophony they agreed to attack Syria, for the Lord would surely give the victory into their hands. Jehoshaphat was not satisfied and wanted a more authoritative prophet to be consulted.

Ahab summoned an officer and charged him to bring the prophet Micaiah, son of Imlah before them. Micaiah was hostile and made fun of the "yes" men of the king. Micaiah pretended to agree with the four hundred prophets.

Ahab became impatient and shouted at Micaiah to tell him the truth!

"Shall we go to Ramoth-Gilead to battle the Syrians or not?"

Micaiah did as Ahab demanded and told the truth.

"I saw all Israel scattered upon the mountains, as sheep that have no shepherd."

Ahab was enraged!

"I told you these prophets will not prophesy anything good for me. Always they portend evil for me.'

Micaiah shook his head in frustration. Then he spoke again.

"Hear the word of the Lord! I saw the Lord sitting on his throne, and all the host of heaven standing beside him, on his right and on his left; and the Lord said, who will entice Ahab, that he may go up and fall at Ramoth-Gilead? One said one thing and one said another. Then a spirit came forward and stood before the Lord saying, 'I will entice him.' The Lord said, 'By what means?' And he said, 'I will go forth and will be a lying spirit in the mouth of all his prophets.'

"So, my kings, there is a lying spirit in the mouths of your prophets! The Lord has spoken that there is an evil concerning you."

Then one of Ahab's prophets struck Micaiah on the side of the head and told him to run and hide but Ahab gave an order.

"Put Micaiah into the prison! He shall be fed nothing but bread and water until I return victorious!"

Jezebel now knew Ahab would not be victorious this time. Strong drink and months of drunkenness had addled Ahab's brain. He was not making good decisions and would most likely be killed. Micaiah might die of starvation, so she sent servants to bring him food. Then she had him released.

I prayed and consulted Astarte as to what I should do. She was silent but I knew she was watching over me. Aishah was there holding me steady.

Ahab and Jehoshaphat gathered their troops and rode off to war together to Syria to take back Ramoth-Gilead. Ahab disguised himself as a common soldier so they would not recognize him. But word went out among the Arameans that the fight was only with Israel and King Ahab, not Judah.

The Arameans went after Jehoshaphat who was in his kingly robes. When the generals saw it was not Ahab, they turned away. But one Aramean soldier shot an arrow striking Ahab in the back.

He shouted to his chariot driver to pull back. But the battle grew intense. The troops charged forward, and there was no retreat. They propped Ahab up in his chariot and sent it charging ahead into the Arameans. In the evening it was obvious he was dead. Then the shout went out to the armies.

"Ahab is dead! Every man go home to his city and every man to his country!"

The troops immediately dispersed and the battle was over. Ahab's body was brought to Samaria to be buried. Ahaziah was now king.

Jezebel had Ahab buried beneath the altar of Baal in the palace temple. Eser and Mattan arrived just in time from Tyre for the burial ceremony and the coronation of Ahaziah.

Jezebel found Ahab's coronation robes and everything she needed. The ceremony was attended by the palace guard and military generals. Eser was the only king who attended. Jehoshaphat was recovering from the battle. Jezebel would be the queen regent until Ahaziah was of age to fully assume the throne.

"I know you have trained him well, my sister. I will stay here and teach these two young men how to be kings. Mattan has been at my side since Laila died. He will be a great help."

"Thank you, Eser. You know I have much to attend to. I am so happy you and Mattan are here. I must admit I was stunned but not surprised when they brought Ahab home. Somehow I knew how it would turn out for him."

"How did it happen?"

"He was always full of wine and decided to go into battle as a common soldier, thinking they would kill King Jehoshaphat of Judah believing it was him. But they recognized the King of Judah and began to withdraw when they saw it was not Ahab. Then a stray arrow hit Ahab. He died in his chariot charging the retreating Syrian enemy."

"How did the battle turn out?"

"At Ahab's death they all turned and went home. It was over."

"King Jehoshaphat did not stay and continue the battle?"

"No, it was all Ahab's idea to attack Syria to restore a city to Israel. Jehoshaphat really had no stake in it except to help Ahab and keep peace between Israel and Judah. I even suspect in the battle Jehoshaphat hung back and all but abandoned Ahab."

"I wish we could abandon all of this, find a camel caravan, and go back to the peaceful life we had."

Jezebel laughed. Possibly the first good laugh she had allowed herself in a very long time.

"For now Ahaziah needs me. Athaliah does not. She will murder all of Judah without my help."

"Would you help her?"

"Perhaps to avenge Ahab's death. One of my first promises to him was to protect him from his enemies. Even after his death I will keep this promise."

Eser immediately took Ahaziah and Mattan to cities where he had diplomatic connections and taught them how to talk to dignitaries at all levels and royalty. He taught them the art of negotiation and peace making.

Upon recovering King Jehoshaphat of Judah made an alliance with young King Ahaziah of Israel. He agreed with him to construct a fleet of trading ships. Ahaziah was thrilled at the thought of having a fleet to sail the Great Sea as his Phoenician family had for generations. He and Mattan would be kings of the sea!

Chapter 49

Ahaziah watched the building of the ships with relish. Every detail was precious to him. He would have the greatest fleet ever to sail the Great Sea. He sent messages to Mattan about the progress.

After the ships were built, Eliezer son of Dodavahu of Mareshah, prophesied against King Jehoshaphat, saying, *"Because you have made an alliance with Ahaziah, a Baal worshipper, the LORD will destroy what you have made."*

He saw to it the ships were wrecked, set afire, and sunk. Ahaziah could not believe his dream of being on the sea was completely destroyed. Horrified, how could he tell Mattan?

Through the frustrating struggles with power and disappointment, Ahaziah changed. He began to drink heavily like his father. Jezebel was alarmed and tried to talk to him. But like Ahab, he turned away from her. Her dear Ahaziah, so like Eser, was breaking her heart.

During one of his many drunken parties, Ahaziah fell from the roof-gallery balcony of the palace. Jezebel and the royal physicians hovered over him administering to his injuries, but he soon died.

There was a hurried coronation of Joram, his younger brother. Jezebel could hardly fathom young Joram was now king of Israel. He had spent most of his days with the military rarely appearing at the palace. It was all so unreal. Jezebel went through the motions of the transfer of power as if in a fog.

The loss of Ahaziah was almost too much. Jezebel was inconsolable. She tended to her duties, holding court, meeting with messengers and diplomats, as one in a trance. She turned to her memoirs for distraction but they were little comfort.

She summoned Joshua to again come and scribe for her.

"These may be short sessions, Joshua. I am not feeling well and will need to rest."

"I am at your service for whatever you need, Your Highness."

"Let us begin."

What a nuisance Israel's prophets are! They are always jumping up in our faces to accuse us of crimes against their god...

Elijah, who is alone now, hides like a coward...

Jezebel stopped after a while and dismissed Joshua. Her anger grew with each word until she began to feel exhausted and ill.

"I am still grieving the loss of my son, Joshua. We will start again soon."

"Yes, Your Highness. I will be ready."

She went to the altars of Baal and Astarte in the palace and prayed for long periods of time. Memories of Aishah and Ashara were fleeting. She tried to hold on to them, but they would quickly fade. She wondered if they were even real any more.

In the cool hours of the early mornings Jezebel went to the stable and had her favorite horse saddled. A retinue of guards rode with her over the hills and countryside. The horses were eager to run. She gave her horse its head to gallop and felt freedom again as the wind blew her hair and robe.

It was in those few hours she could almost forget the terrible things that were happening to her life. It reminded her of riding along the Tigris River with Eser, Hannibal, and Barek. Those memories would bring tears and longing. But longing for what? She could never go back.

Jezebel sent young Athaliah to Jerusalem for her wedding. Jezebel did not go with her. Jerusalem was too volatile toward her. She would be a distraction or worse be murdered.

Athaliah did not care who attended. She just wanted to get the festivities over with. This marriage was an abomination to her, being forced to marry this creepy Prince Jehoram.

King Jehoshaphat died and was buried in Jerusalem. His son Jehoram, Athaliah's husband, became king. Jehoram went on a bloody rampage killing all his brothers and their families so they could not challenge him for the throne.

Queen Athaliah was determined to survive King Jehoram's murderous plots that might one day include her and her yet unborn child. She began to plan her own ascension to the throne of Judah. There were those in the court and army who hated Jehoram as much as she did. They were more than willing to join in her plans for his demise and all of his despicable allies. It would not be soon, but it would come.

Jezebel's concentration was still a little scattered. She wanted to get her story written, so reluctantly she continued her memoirs again for a short time. Joshua was always eager to scribe for her. He was fascinated by her story. His enthusiasm was a bright spot in her day.

"Are you ready, Joshua?"

"Yes, Your Highness. I am ready."

We fought and won a war against Ben-hadad, King of Syria…

Ahab should have killed him…

Ahab was forgiving, which makes him very popular with the people…

Naboth, could not sell the vineyard that had belonged to his family for generations…

The time was dragging by and Jezebel had a hard time keeping focused on what had happened. Images of Ahaziah lying on the courtyard stones kept coming to her mind.

"That is all Joshua. Please go. We will continue again later."

Young King Joram ruled twelve years. In that time he tore down the stone image his father had made to honor Baal, and tried to do what was right in the sight of the lord. He had no training in the ways of Yahweh. He continued going to war with Moab and Syria.

Jezebel despaired of the wreckage of war and deaths of thousands of young men in the military. The peace of Phoenicia was nowhere to be found. The images of Baal and Asherahs of Astarte were torn down. Another precious part of her life was slipping away. All that had formed her younger life, the beliefs and all that made her strong, were in ashes.

She sent a message to Eser she planned to come to Tyre. He sent a message back saying he would be happy to welcome her. She was relieved he would be there and she left Samaria immediately.

It was such a relief to cross into Phoenicia. She could feel her sadness lift with each mile toward Tyre. Eser met her and they threw their arms around each other.

"Come and tell me all that has happened, my dear sister. Your message sounded as if you have been in a war with yourself."

"I truly have, Eser. I have lost Aishah and all she means to me. I feel like a hollow shell of a person, filled with anger and hate. I might have jumped off the ship into the deep water coming back from Auza if I had known how terrible it would all be."

"There is a ship leaving for Byblos in the morning and we will be on it. We must visit Ashara and the School of Astarte to heal our hearts and regain our balance."

Chapter 50

"Oh, Eser, I am such a wreck! I fear to have them see me this way. My hair is graying. I feel old and drained."

"You are still my beautiful sister. Tonight we will talk, read messages from Hannibal and Barek about their cities, and sleep. Tomorrow the sea air will refresh us and Byblos will welcome us. Do not worry."

Early in the morning they went to the docks of Tyre and boarded the ship. The sea breezes whipped around them as the oarsmen backed it out of the berth and turned it into the seaway.

"I am on a ship and I am home! If there is a camel caravan close to Byblos, I may disappear forever."

They laughed, reminisced, and sat quietly together basking in each other's presence. Jezebel could feel the life coming back into her limbs and coursing through her whole being.

The welcome sight of the School of Astarte was before them. Jezebel envisioned Ashara coming to greet them as she always had, but she was not there. Jezebel was almost in a panic.

"Where is Ashara? Is she not here?"

"Yes, Aishah, she is here. I will take you to her."

"You know who I am, priestess?"

"Oh yes! You are revered here forever. We keep you in our prayers every day."

Ashara and Aishah rushed into each other's arms. Eser held the both of them and tears rolled down all their cheeks.

"Are you well, Ashara?"

"Yes, I am…just getting a little older. But life is good and they take good care of me here. Come…there is a place prepared for us at the inn where we can all be together."

They walked to the inn where Eser had stayed and where Ashara taught him about energies and cosmic dimensions.

"You must help me find Aishah. I have lost her through all the trials and troubles I experienced these many years in Samaria. I have tried and tried but I cannot do it alone. I just feel empty."

"Aishah is still there. We will find our way through the hard shell of outer experiences and you will see. She is there."

They talked and studied through the days. Late in the evenings Ashara and Aishah returned to the school, indulged in fragrant baths, ate light snacks, and slept in each other's arms as they used to do.

They went to the temple for morning vespers and walked to the inn to meet Eser.

"Eser walks with a slight limp and his hair is graying too. Has he been well?"

"Yes. Laila's death was difficult for him. His son, Mattan, seems to be a capable king, so he is at peace."

"I must admit, I have missed him. My days are not so busy since the younger priestesses have taken over the duties of the school. Most of the work has gotten too much for me."

Eser had a longing in his eyes as he met them each morning when they broke their fast together. Aishah watched as he sat down closer to Ashara. Surprising them both he took her hand.

"Ashara, would you consider coming back to Tyre with me? Could we finish out our lives together and enjoy the companionship that destiny has denied us all these years?"

Ashara thought for a few minutes and smiled at him.

"Yes, I will love to come and be with you."

After a few weeks they boarded a Phoenician ship. Eser spoke to the captain and the captain was nodding. Jezebel became curious.

"What was that about, Eser?"

"We have a surprise in store for us! We are going to Auza. The ship going to Tyre is not yet here, so we will take this one."

"Auza? Great Astarte, Eser! Auza?"

"How are you at sea, Ashara? Have you been on a ship?"

"Yes, once a very long time ago. It was a pleasant experience after someone put a potion in my wine to keep my stomach calm."

"I will see there is some on board if you should need it."

It was many years since Jezebel had been on a ship to Auza. This was a faster ship than she remembered their ships being. The ports and stops at dusk for the night seemed to fly by. The waters were calm for which they were thankful. Ashara weathered it very well.

Her eagerness to see Auza and Hannibal energized her days until at last they arrived. There was a white haired elderly man sitting on the dock chatting with the workers.

"Hannibal? Hannibal is that you?"

"It is I, yes, and who are you? I do not see well these days."

"It is Jezebel!"

"Great Astarte! Jezebel! I thought I would never see you again. Well, I cannot see you very well now, but come closer."

She ran and embraced him.

"Eser is with me and our friend and teacher, Ashara from the School of Astarte."

The reunion was happy and sad at the same time. Anah and Juha had both died of an illness, but Hannibal had a son, Hiram.

"He runs our city now. I do what I can…mostly advise. We will come to the inn for dinner this evening with you. Blessed Astarte, I did not think this could ever be!"

Jezebel avoided going over the details of her life in Samaria. She had told Eser and Ashara and that was enough. She wanted to bask in the glow of being with Hannibal, meeting Hiram, and looking over Auza. They placed flowers at the tomb of Anah and Juha, and toured the city in a carriage with Hannibal.

Chapter 51

Hiram was a most engaging and knowledgeable young man, happy to share his city with them. Jezebel smiled. *Of course it is now his city. He was born here. Hannibal and I are past being able to care for it and happy to give it into his capable hands.*

Eser and Ashara left the carriage and wandered into the markets together. Jezebel and Hannibal drove to the shore.

"I know, Jezebel, many things have been very difficult for you in Samaria. News travels even as far as Auza. I think of you often."

She laid her head down on his still massive shoulder and cried. She could not stop the grief from pouring out.

"I am sorry…"

"Just cry it out, my love. It has been a long time coming, I am sure."

As her sobs eventually subsided, they sat quietly together, letting the sea breezes dry their tears. It was so good to be in the safety of Hannibal's presence and bask in the love that always underscored their years together.

"I was a brat, Hannibal."

"Yes, you were. My favorite kind."

They burst out laughing.

He turned the carriage back toward the inn. Jezebel was sure Eser and Ashara had returned to it already. After dinner Eser and Ashara went to their room and Jezebel and Hannibal went to hers.

There was a supreme happiness in the inn that night. How long it would last until destiny's cold grip took over again, they did not know. But now tonight was all that mattered.

The next week the Phoenician ship was ready to leave the harbor. Hannibal decided to accompany Jezebel back to Tyre and return to Auza on the next trading ship. He knew she was dreading this trip back to Samaria. She would not be coming back and he would never see her again. This would be the last voyage they would take together.

Ashara told Eser she had terrible foreboding about Jezebel.

"We should never have allowed her to go back to Samaria alone. Destiny is closing in on her and we should be there."

"What can we do? She would not allow us to go back with her. She wanted us to stay in Tyre and live happily here. But are you saying we should go now?"

"Soon, my dear Eser. We can travel quietly and not attract attention. Two old people on a holy quest."

"We will not tell Mattan. He would want to send a retinue of guards with us."

"Perhaps we should tell Mattan. The guards could go as far as the city and we would walk in as peasants. King Jehu is on a murderous rampage. We may need protection getting though the countryside."

"It is dangerous either way. But I agree. We must go. We cannot desert Jezebel now."

King Mattan was not happy, but he knew they would go. He did not have an army to send into Samaria with them. A small group of guards would have to do.

"We will send you by ship from Tyre to the Port of Dor just past Mount Carmel. From there you will travel east to the city of Samaria and the palace."

"We need horses so we can move quickly."

Mattan's guards helped them plan a route to travel off the main roads through the hills. It would be only twenty three miles from the shore to the palace in Samaria.

"It might be a little rough but there are people who will guide you along the way. They are part of the Phoenician guard who occupy outposts and report to us. We will notify them."

"Thank you, Mattan. We appreciate all you are willing to do to help us. Do not worry. We are older and do not fear death. It is likely no one will bother two old people on a holy quest to Mount Carmel."

"I know what Aunt Jezebel means to you and you have my blessing. Be careful and return safely."

Ashara hugged Mattan and blessed him.

"You are a truly noble and courageous son. Astarte willing we will return."

They took a smaller ship out of Tyre to the Port of Dor which was just south of Mount Carmel. Rather than horses, there were asses waiting for them. A member of the Phoenician guard stood by holding their bridles.

"I know you requested horses but we have none that can serve you at this time. The asses are gentle, swift, and surefooted. They are well trained and faithful to their riders. They will stay near you. They are the better choice, King Eser. I hope you are not displeased. It would take several days to procure horses."

Eser knew the temperament of the ass and was pleased at the guard's choice. Several days to get horses might make them too late.

"It is Astarte watching over us, Eser. It is a blessing."

The guard drew a crude map of a way through the hills of Samaria. He noted where the passes were to easily get past higher elevations. The hills of Samaria were not mountains, but knowing the location of the passes would make travel easier. He also marked a village that would welcome them if they needed assistance. A few of the Phoenician guards lived in the villages.

"Thank you for your help. May Astarte and King Mattan will richly reward you."

They started off in the late afternoon so it would be almost dark when they reached Samaria and the palace. There would be a bright moon to light their way.

Jezebel walked into the palace in Samaria to find things in disarray. Her work lay where she left it and the people were clamoring at the gates for an audience. The servants wandered about seeming to be lost and lifeless. Was it really her presence there that gave it life and kept everything functioning?

She rang for Joshua and presently he appeared with his writing materials.

"I am so glad to see you, Your Highness! We have all felt a little lost without you."

"You may be the only one who is happy to see me, Joshua. What has happened here?"

Chapter 52

S he regretted putting it on Joshua's shoulders to explain and apologized to him. He blushed a little and immediately set to work. He read the last entry to her so she could pick up the thread of where she left off.

For days Ahab raged and ranted over that vineyard. Then he would sit mute for hours refusing to speak. Angry and sullen he would not eat or sleep...
   My plan to frighten Naboth into giving up the vineyard was simple...
   I did not expect things to go that far, and I regretted Naboth was among the dead. It was not in my plan.

   'Ahab! Stop shouting. I did not murder anyone or intend anyone should die. The Jews did that...
   Now go! Claim your vineyards and be happy!'

   Elijah was aghast at the news and his shouting could be heard all the way to the palace...
   Ahab cowered as he always did before Elijah...
   I offered him a good price, two vineyards of twice the size! He had no reason to deny me. I am the king...!
   Naboth and several others are dead! Murdered, Ahab, by your queen and with your permission! You knew what she would do...'
   I never asked her to kill Naboth...

Joshua was a little wide-eyed at this story. He had been calm, concentrating on his writing, but now he was finding it hard to maintain his composure.

"Joshua, you look a little pale. Perhaps you should rest and we will continue later on."

"Yes, Your Majesty, I do need some rest. I am very sorry."

"No need to be sorry. I am ready to stop as well. Have a restful night."

Joshua collected his writing materials, bowed deeply, and left the room.

News came that Aiziah, Athaliah's son, was dead. Athaliah had flown into a murderous rage. She gathered her supporters and they killed all the members of the Royal House of Judah. In a coup she took the throne of Judah for herself and became the first woman to rule Judah.

Jezebel sat down on a chaise. She had a terrible foreboding and now dark dreams assailed her at night. Exhausted she felt a darkness closing around her.

My daughter, Athaliah, is a murderess! Her son Aiziah is dead! My son Ahaziah is dead! Ahab was killed because of Jehoshaphat! And Joram? Will he live? And me..."

Her heart was pounding. She fainted on the chaise and rolled off onto the floor. She woke up to her servants bathing her face and calling to her. They helped her to her feet and she sat down on the chaise to compose herself.

"Here, Your Highness, sip some wine."

Jezebel took the goblet and looked at it doubtfully. She took a sip and immediately felt a little better. It became clear she must finish her memoirs before her life is taken too.

"Joshua! Bring me Joshua."

The servants ran from her room to get Joshua. Jezebel, still a little shaky, went to her outer room to wait for him. Thoughts were racing through her mind as she paced the floor. Joshua ran in breathless.

"Your Highness! I am here!"

"Good, Joshua. Let us begin..."

The day came that my priests had been preparing for many months. Special altars were built and firewood gathered for each one...

I fell on my knees calling on Astarte to avenge me and rid the land of this viper...

The showdown came and Elijah seemed larger than life...

I retreated to the palace and waited...

At Elijah's word, or by some secret magic, he kindled the fire and ordered his people to slay my priests by the Kishon brook...!

It was still raining and Elijah took Ahab up onto Mount Carmel to eat and drink with him. Ahab cowered before Elijah while Elijah cursed him...

Then he eventually stole away back to the palace and to me...

Jezebel's mood became black as a storm. While she stalked around the room, Joshua kept to his work as best he could. For the first time he began to fear he was in danger. Her moods swung wildly and he could no longer predict her actions. He was afraid to just excuse himself and leave her presence.

Jezebel saw his distress. She smiled at him and touched his shoulder.

"Be at peace, Joshua. All is well. We will continue."

Then Elijah came toward the gates of the city, but Ahab got here first and I told him the priests of Ba'al were all dead...

All was peaceful since I rid Israel of Elijah. Even Israel and Syria were three years without war...

Jezebel was exhausted and dismissed Joshua. He was relieved to go.

She paced in the tower of her palace. She looked out over the Jezreel Valley. The olive orchards stretched all the way east to the Jordan. She looked westward toward the fertile plain ending at Mount Carmel. There was her beloved Great Sea that had taken her so many wonderful places.

Even though it all looked so peaceful, Jezebel knew there was a ground swell coming against her since she had banished Elijah.

She had freely spread her religion without restraint which was her right. The Jews were incensed at the licentiousness of her new priests. They

213

considered the naked statues to be shameful. All of these things were an abomination in their eyes.

There is no food or water in those hills and I am sure Elijah will die a slow agonizing death. So I have called the guards back and left him for dead. What do I do now? Everyone is gone. I am alone.

Chapter 53

Jezebel called Joshua back. Fearfully he came with his writing brush and ink, and fresh papyrus. Jezebel ignored his nervousness and began.

Ahab convinced Jehoshaphat to go into the battle in his royal robes, while Ahab would disguise himself...

I am told an archer recognized Ahab by his armor and shot him with an arrow...

The enemy troops retreated to their homes and their own countries. Ahab's war and his life were over...

Jehoram, whose wife is Athaliah, my daughter, was king and there were revolts everywhere...

For twelve years now this has gone on. Wars, defeats, starvation, and wreckage everywhere...

Assyria now rises against us again and I am told King Jehu is riding furiously toward my palace to take my life...

Joshua was terrified. He gathered all of his writings and ran from the room. He hurried down to the kitchen in the servants' quarters and pushed the memoirs into the blazing hearth. Even though he was out of breath from panic and running, he stayed and watched to be sure they were consumed.

He went to his father and told him about burning the memoirs.

"Was I right to do that, Father? I was afraid King Jehu would find them. I made sure they were completely in ashes."

"You saved our lives, Joshua. King Jehu would surely kill us if we are found with them."

"But her story…"

"It will never be told unless perhaps someday you will write it again when we are all in a safer place."

They both left the palace by the servants' entrance and took a back way far into the hills.

King Jehu executed King Joram by shooting him in the back with an arrow and had his body thrown into the vineyard that had belonged to Naboth. It was punishment because his parents' had caused Naboth's death and stolen his land.

Eser and Ashara arrived at the palace. A frightened servant pointed them to the tower. Jezebel turned from her reverie to see them coming up the circular stone steps.

"My dear sister, what can we do for you? We can take you to the Port of Dor with us and home to Tyre."

The three of them held each other for a moment.

"Great Astarte, you have risked your lives coming here!"

"Come with us now!"

"I cannot, my beloved ones. King Jehu will hunt me down wherever I am and you will be killed too. He will destroy Phoenicia. It is better that it ends here. Go back before it is too late. Go now."

Eser and Ashara knew she was right. There was no way they could save her. They had to go back to save Phoenicia and King Mattan.

"Aishah! We will be close by and raise our vibrations to light of the Highest Heaven. When your moment comes, do the same."

"I will come to the large window. You will see me there. I will raise Aishah's vibration of light. Thanks to you I know she is still here within me. I love you!"

They tearfully hugged her, hurried back down the spiral stairs, ran down to the servants' quarters and out of the palace.

The servants who had already left the palace and were just outside motioned to them to follow.

"We want to stay close by. Where can we hide?"

"There is a side doorway into a crypt where you will not be seen. There are empty jars. King Jehu will come to a place just around the corner under the large window. The window is where proclamations are made. She will come there."

Eser and Ashara pulled their hoods over their heads and covered their faces. They found the doorway and crouched down in the shadows to wait.

Jezebel ran through the halls shouting for the servants, but she found the palace deserted. She quickly dressed herself in her formal robes and crown as the royal Queen of Israel.

Ahab had been gone for ten years. Mattan was now King of Phoenicia. Athaliah had murdered the Royal Family of Judah and seized the throne for herself.

King Jehu has just murdered my whole family, even Joram, and there is nothing left for me but death. My destiny is complete.

Jezebel walked to the window of the palace. At King Jehu's demand she stepped to the window. She stood tall as the Queen of Israel. Her jewelry glittered gold. Her face was radiant in the setting sun.

She called down to him in a commanding voice.

"King Jehu, coward! Like dead King Zimri, you will also suffer his fate. He was on the throne only one week. And now destiny is coming for you as well! You will live a terrible life of war and death."

She looked down at him. He refused to look up at her.

"Coward! You look at the ground where you belong with the other dogs! You do not dare look up at me!"

"Push her down! Or I will kill all of you!"

Eser and Ashara were huddled in the dark corner dressed as a paupers praying to Astarte when they saw Jezebel appear in the window of the palace.

They joined their light into one great ball of cosmic fire. Jezebel saw it and joined them by raising every atom of her being to the highest vibration with all the power Aishah and Jezebel, eternally united, could muster.

The light exploded all around her. Immediately there was a fire on the ground below the window. Jezebel was gone.

When the crowds turned and ran, Eser and Ashara tearfully gathered the ashes and remains of her skull, feet, and hands into an urn and stole away in the night.

The asses were still waiting where they left them as the Phoenician had promised. They arrived safely at the Port of Dor and took the waiting ship back to Tyre. Jezebel's remains were ceremoniously hidden in the tomb of Queen Laila, where they would rest as sisters in spirit forever.

The servants in the palace at Samaria returned and set out a banquet for King Jehu and his generals. After he had eaten and was quite drunk, he told the servants to go and bury Jezebel's body since she was a king's daughter.

The servants returned and reported there was no body. All they found were ashes.

"Ashes?"

King Jehu was drunk and dangerously enraged.

"Go back and look again you fools! Someone must have stolen her body! I will burn whoever did this! Find her!"

Terrified the servants ran out of the palace and toward the hills. One of King Jehu's guards stopped them, sword drawn.

"Who are you and where are you going?"

"King Jehu send us to bury the body of Queen Jezebel. Please take a message to the king that it is done."

The guard immediately went into the palace to deliver the message. The servants ran into the hills and were gone, never to return.

Joshua always regretted having to destroy Jezebel's memoirs. He thought about the contents often and tried to remember all he could. His father passed away. Now the memoirs could no longer bring danger to him.

News came that King Jehu was killed. Queen Athaliah was taken from the throne of Judah in a coup and murdered. There was no one left now who could threaten him.

Now an old man he sat outside of his hut near the Port of Dor with a pile of papyrus, his ink and favorite brush, and began to write all he remembered. He knew how it began and the rest tucked away in his mind would surely follow.

"I am Queen Jezebel…"